BERTIONI'S HOTEL

BERTIONI'S HOTEL

by
JEAN NICOL

London
MICHAEL JOSEPH

First published in Great Britain by Michael Joseph Ltd
44 Bedford Square, London WC1B 3DU
1983
© 1983 by Jean Nicol

ISBN 0 7181 2218 6

Typeset by MHL Typesetting Ltd, Coventry.
Printed in Great Britain by
Hollen Street Press Ltd, Slough
and bound by Hunter & Foulis Ltd, Edinburgh

To
HUGH WONTNER

LIST OF HOTEL STAFF MENTIONED IN
BERTIONI'S HOTEL

Sir Adrian Wearne	Chairman of Hotel Regina
Carlo Bertioni	Managing Director
Andrew Merrin	General Manager
Major Salter	Assistant Manager
Spiros	Night Manager
Tom Raffin	Publicity Director
Nancy Smith-Bretherton	Assistant to Publicity Director
Raymond	Grill Room Manager
Pieter	Deputy Grill Room Manager
Guiseppe	Reception Manager
Crispen	Receptionist
Garbin	Banqueting Manager
Robin Wearne	Bill Office Clerk
(son of Sir Adrian)	

Ex-Hotel Regina Staff	
Moxon	Head Porter
Miss Ballater	Head Florist
Lobb	Head of Works Department
Pierre	Banqueting Manager
Monsieur Le Brun	Maître Chef of the Restaurant Kitchen

All the characters in this book are entirely fictitious

ONE

There was an air of festivity about the Hotel Regina unusual for a Sunday evening. Figures that seemed familiar, but older, greyer, stooped under heavy overcoats, made their way to the gentleman's cloakroom. Only Moxon, wearing his short raincoat with the air of a British Warm, stood erect as ever, shoulders back, shoes polished to black enamel.

It was some years since he had retired as Head Porter, leaving his desk by the revolving doors to a younger man who read the *Daily Mirror* instead of the social columns of *The Times*, and did not have eyes in the back of his head or that instant awareness of everything that was happening in the Front Hall. Moxon could sense the Manager, Mr Bertioni, without looking up, knew he stood at the head of the stairs looking down on his world, immobile, the first to see the fallen petal from the flower arrangement in the foyer, the unemptied ash-tray, the page boy shuffling on the bench at the back of the Enquiry Office. Moxon noted these things too. To him they had been the pulse of life; and now, retired in a comfortable suburban bungalow, it was still the grey and white tiled foyer he saw when he lay awake in the early hours, and the swathe of violet carpet stretching towards the bar, the panelled walls palely lit by candelabra, black-polished counters indicating the Reception and Enquiry Offices, upholstered sofas facing glass-topped tables, writing desks in secluded corners with neat squares of hotel stationery, the scent and colour of massed flowers and, dominating it all, the great curved staircase down which Bertioni would eventually descend, pale chiselled face like a marble statue; and with the wave of an impatient hand, he'd start an immediate flurry of activity.

Today was Bertioni's 75th birthday and they were all gathered, the old servants and the new. Typical of him, thought Moxon, to have been born so that it came on a Sunday, the quietest day of the hotel week, the Restaurant closed and the Grill half empty, but the largest banqueting room ablaze with lights.

Moxon handed in his raincoat, recognising the slight figure of Pierre, the former Banqueting Manager, beside him, wearing his dinner jacket as if he had been born in it, his white hair newly washed, fluffy as dandelion seeds.

"Evening, Pierre. At least we've still got our hair!" Moxon was jovial, pulling at his moustache, rather sparse now and tinged with tobacco stains.

"I suppose you have already looked in the Gainsborough Room and found all not to your liking?"

Pierre's answering smile was a wan affair. He had a pear-shaped face, broad forehead, ribbed like sea-sand, tired eyes behind gold-rimmed spectacles, a network of peevish scribbles etched round a thin mouth.

"Not what it was. I looked in on the way and that new Banqueting Manager—Garbage—"

"Garbin," interrupted Moxon, who liked to keep in touch.

"Well, whatever his name is he wasn't there," Pierre continued. "Should have been there from the start, get the atmosphere right. No standards now," he grumbled, "just waiters jostling and giggling, probably pinching the drinks, for all I know."

"Oh, come on," said Moxon good humouredly, "that doesn't happen here. What you need is a good drink yourself. Let's go in the staff bar, we've got time."

"We aren't staff any more," Pierre sighed.

"Of course we are, always will be. Why have we been invited to the birthday party tonight if we're not?"

"Probably won't let us in."

"Let them try," Moxon squared his shoulders, leading the

way. What a dreary old man Pierre had become; difficult to remember his past skirmishes now. There was that girl from the florist's, proper little tart, in and out of the Banqueting Manager's office between courses . . .

"Flowers weren't as good as your Miss Ballater's either," Pierre said, following Moxon's broad back through the baize door into an eruption of noise.

Moxon ordered large scotches, noticed the barman was young and amiable, and looked round for old friends. Seeing no one, he collected the drinks and went back to Pierre.

"What about the flowers?" he asked, remembering the 'your' Miss Ballater. Yes, he had become fond of her, seeing behind the sharp manner and the apparent lack of warmth, a woman devoted to her job and to the standards that were so dear to him. Cut above him, of course; her uncle a bishop, and wearing shapeless tweeds to Covent Garden in the early hours with an insolence he recognised but found hard to understand.

"Pink chrysanthemums, that's what," answered Pierre, "great tiers of them. Bertioni never did like chrysanthemums." He sighed. "That's what comes of having a shop doing the flowers. Miss Ballater would have known."

He drained his glass and nodded towards a nearby table.

"Norman Lobb's over there. Lost a lot of weight. Looks like an empty sack. Used to be such a big fellow, always the first to move the trestles and put up the tables; changed the top table sometimes half a dozen times before we got it the right size; and Norman always up there giving orders, but doing it himself as well." He paused, looking at his empty glass.

"Time for the other half?"

Moxon shook his head.

"No—one more, then it will be two and we'll be late. Wouldn't do."

He was aware he was back to sergeant major, but Pierre accepted without argument and followed Moxon down the gold-carpeted passage.

3

"Not such good quality as the last one," Pierre was grumbling again, scuffling his toe into the pile. "Used to be two inches thick in the old days."

"Well, at least they've gone back to this colour. Remember that jazzy red white and blue stuff?"

"And those plastic white chairs like egg cups in the private rooms? No wonder Norman decided he'd had enough being Works Manager. Bad time that was. Wonder what he'll say in his speech tonight?"

"Talk of the old days, I expect. He felt safe then. I suppose we all did." Moxon smoothed his moustache. "Knew what we were working for and took a pride in it."

Ahead of them, black backs marked the end of a slow-moving queue and, joining it, Moxon peered ahead, hoping to see a flash of colour. What would Miss Ballater be wearing? Long skirt and blouse, most likely. Hair would be grey now, but those bony features would not have collected soft folds. He remembered suddenly the warm day when, looking across from his desk to the flower kiosk on the other side of the revolving doors, he had seen her flushed, pushing back damp strands of hair and, catching her eye, had walked over and suggested a drink.

In her tweed suit and white blouse, the Head Florist became more intimidating when he was near her, and Moxon regretted his impulse.

"Far too warm in here," Miss Ballater had appeared irritated. "Look at these tulips," adding, "and you know women aren't allowed in the staff bar."

"I didn't mean here," and Moxon had suggested the Turnpike on the corner of the square. "One of your girls could come up." And to his surprise she had accepted.

The scent of lilac from the gardens had been sweet in the sunlight as he walked round the square. There'd been a moment of anxiety, but as he'd pushed open the green door of the pub into the shade and faint smell of detergent inside, he had known what to order. Not beer, or lager, but a large gin and tonic for both of them—with ice, of course, and a slice of lemon; and a table in the corner of the private bar.

She had arrived a few minutes later, letting in a square of sunlight from the pavement as he carried the glasses from the bar.

It had been the right choice and a good beginning, though he had never called her anything but Miss Ballater—until, after their drinks at the corner table had become a ritual, he had taken her to the theatre and to Rules for dinner. There, relaxed against the plush banquette, Miss Ballater had said: "My name is Rowenna—but never in the hotel," she had added crisply.

Moxon nodded. They understood each other.

Moxon found himself at the head of the queue. Already Pierre was bending over Mrs Bertioni's hand, kissing it with an expertise he had perfected over the years. George Peters from Swansea, but Pierre had sounded and proved better, thought Moxon with a wry smile, turning to give his name to the toast master.

"Mr Moxon."

Even a sergeant major could not have done better. Bertioni turned and smiled. It was a pleased smile. Here you all are, my old friends and comrades. We saw it all together, the phoney war, the blitz, and the years that followed; not the years we had expected, but we did keep going knowing what we believed in. Yes, we kept going, thought Bertioni, and we remembered the past and what men fought for, and how it should have been.

"Congratulations and happy birthday," said Moxon, shaking hands and noticing, as he always had done, Bertioni's long elegant fingers.

"It is good to see you—the old faces mean so much to me," Bertioni said, then leaned forward to add quietly: "Let us have a drink together later on. You remember my wife, of course? Beryl, my dear."

Beside the slim grace of Bertioni, she seemed a small bundle

5

of powder blue; soft round face, fine white hair teased into curls.

"Oh, I do remember you so well in your pulpit," said Beryl. "That was Louise, of course, always called your little round desk your pulpit. Such a lovely girl, but she's always been her father's favourite—she can do no wrong." The small mouth, smudged and a little moist, turned down, then suddenly she brightened. "My grandson is married now."

"Yes, I had heard," Moxon replied politely, seeing her eyes slide back to Bertioni and the stranger who was behind him.

It was like Shangri La, Moxon thought. Once outside the insularity of the hotel, and you became a hundred. Bertioni, slim, arrogant as ever, ivory, high-boned face, hair now receding—but with style—and the two wings above his ears a silvery grey, looked as he had done ten years ago—better, perhaps. There was a curious alchemy about the Regina. Stay here, working, forget the outside world and you'd stay stamped, marked in your job as you are now, unchanged. Mrs Bertioni, who had never understood the confines of the hotel world and escaped whenever she could, was an old lady. Bertioni would protect her, of course, he always had in an odd way, though frequently he was impatient. But how had she kept him all the years?

"Bertioni has a mistress," had been the staff bar gossip.

"Yes, her name's Regina!" But beneath the instant laughter there had been a feeling of pleasure among the older ones that Bertioni's passion was for the hotel alone.

"Champagne, Sir?"

Moxon, hesitating, looked round the room, pinkly lit, warm, vibrating to the surge of voices.

"Probably prefer a scotch like me, eh Moxon?"

The Regina's Chairman turned to the waiter, balancing his party tray. "Get someone to bring two large scotches right away."

Authority. For once Moxon had missed it, but then to him the Chairman of the Hotel Regina had always been Sir John

6

Worsfield. His nephew Adrian, knighted last year for his services to the hotel industry, had been Chairman now for many years, but to Moxon he was still young Adrian Wearne. Florid, broken veins across his cheeks, but personable, very personable, with friendly creases radiating from his eyes and better looking now that he had lost weight riding to hounds twice a week.

"Always think champagne's a morning drink, myself." Sir Adrian was affable, almost intimate.

As if I trot round to the pub for Möet every morning, Moxon smiled to himself, but accepted the speedily brought glass with gratitude.

"You know, Moxon," no condescension now, "my uncle thought a great deal of you."

"I think we knew the rules then." Moxon was moved, and watched the Chairman's face, hoping for further intimacies. But instead, with a great heave of laughter, Sir Adrian waved his glass upwards.

"I forgot. Happy birthday to my father-in-law! And I hope you lot aren't going to sing that awful dirge."

"Of course not," said Moxon stiffly, on his dignity. "He would hate it."

"So he would. That makes two of us. Can't stand that 'happy birthday to you' business. Can't stand birthdays anyway now, eh Moxon?"

Moxon wondered how to steer the conversation back to Sir John, a hard man, with the cold blue eyes of a Siamese cat; a man who had built up and run the Hotel Regina on military lines, of rank and keeping one's place; lines that Moxon understood.

"Well, Moxon, I mustn't keep you. Lots of old friends to see, I expect. Nice to see you looking so fit. Splendid, splendid." Sir Adrian patted Moxon on the shoulder. "Must find my wife and talk to her about the presentation. Have you seen it yet? 18th century chiming clock. Very fine piece."

He's really becoming a caricature, thought Moxon, watching the retreating back, the pale hair, neither blond nor grey, fashionably long and curled over the back of his collar. But the Regina might have done worse. Sir John would have been far too rigid and would have hung on, refusing to sell out to the American company as his nephew had done. Moxon remembered how against it he had been at the time, but the Regina was threadbare and war-damaged and desperately in need of money. And it had worked out better than he had feared, with Adrian Wearne remaining as Chairman and, more important, Bertioni being made Managing Director.

"You can't possibly look so serious at Daddy's birthday party!"

"Miss Louise!" Moxon's pleasure ran through him, warming.

"I'm sorry, I should say Lady Wearne now." He shook her hand. "I always think of you as Miss Louise, forgive me."

"Oh, but I love 'Miss Louise'. Please go on calling me that —makes me feel young. It's rather an old party tonight, isn't it?" she whispered confidingly, "all that 'forty years on when rheumaticky of shoulder' stuff! That's why I love being called Miss Louise—reminds me of coming home from school with my satchel crammed with books." She laughed. "And you always insisted on taking it from me at the entrance and giving it to a page boy!"

Her laughter was infectious. It always had been, Moxon thought, smiling and feeling happy.

"Mr Moxon," she would call, pigtails stiff under felt school hat, pushing the revolving doors round twice for the fun of it, "I've got two sweeties in one of these hands—guess which and they are for you." Dark eyes looked earnestly upwards. "It's alright, they're wrapped in paper." Two clenched fists, one pushed slightly more forward than the other.

Moxon always chose this one.

"Wrong again!" Delighted squeals of laughter. "But, I'm going to give you one of mine."

An odd upbringing for a child—a flat in a luxury hotel, waited on by right because your father is the Manager. Her brother Paul had never been so exuberant—prep school, public school; then, still in his teens, killed landing on a practice flight with the RAF.

She smelt delicious. Had she aged? Was she still beautiful? She was looking across his shoulder, wide mouth parted, eyes very dark and almost—Moxon wondered—tender, perhaps? Her hair was swept upwards but untidily, as if a breeze had blown it that way, and still that pale almost primrose colour. Women were lucky, thought Moxon, they never needed to become grey.

"Well?" Louise said, suddenly smiling up at him. "What is your verdict?"

She laughed at his discomfiture. "Oh, come on, my friend, you have been trying to make up your mind."

Moxon remembered, she liked to call everyone 'my friend'. Mr Moxon would have been too formal, Moxon too patronising. She had always been like that; gay, happy and wanting everyone to share life with her. Never understood why she married young Wearne. Of course, they all said it was a catch, Manager's daughter marrying the Chairman's nephew and heir elect, but he had never felt that. When young Wearne had been pulled out of the Norway fjords more dead than alive in that icy water and flown to Scotland, she had raced to the hospital to see him. And when she came back they were engaged; though Moxon had always felt this was more out of affection and gladness for his recovery than love. War did that to people; played on their sympathies, shutting their eyes to the years ahead.

TWO

The young receptionist on duty fingered his black tie and looked up at the ornate clock on the wall behind him. He was a management trainee in his early twenties and had not been long at the Regina. Tonight was the first time he had been left in charge on the evening shift and he looked round the softly lit foyer, now comfortably restored to its Sunday evening calm, and wished he was taller.

"Deference and a pleasant manner are more important," he had been told; but waiting to greet the President of Lincoln Hotels, the American company which owned the Regina, he stretched upwards, shoulders back, and yearned for those extra inches.

"Mr Jeudwine does not believe in personalities in his hotels," the Reception Manager, Mr Guiseppe, had said. "He feels every job in every department should be interchangeable, that we should all be the same, like the backs of playing cards. I agree with him. So tonight when he arrives from the airport, you will conduct him personally to the President's suite, and I shall be at Mr Bertioni's birthday party."

Guiseppe, who was slim and appeared taller than he was, had brushed-back dark hair; almost too long but well cut, not by the hotel barber, but by a trendy establishment in Jermyn Street.

"Don't forget Mr Jeudwine is likely to bring someone with him; he usually does. There is a suite reserved on the same floor in that event."

Left to himself, the receptionist, who had ambitions and was eager, found the booking; suite 234 and 5 on the opposite side of the corridor from the President's suite. Now standing there, waiting, he wondered if there were flowers and iced water; and as he reached for the telephone to ask for the house-keeper, the familiar sounds of activity at the entrance stopped him. Swift commands, the sound of suitcases brushing the doors, a high American voice.

"Well, where is everybody?"

A forceful, elderly figure, vicuna coat slung carelessly over a light suit, the inevitable cigar. Eyes bright in a face creased as worn corduroy, white hair combed carefully across a broad forehead.

"You're new. Do you know who I am?"

"Of course, Mr Jeudwine, we are expecting you. I hope you had a good flight?"

"This place is like a morgue," grumbled the American, noting the young round face and new jacket. "Where is everybody?" he repeated. "Are you in charge?"

"Yes, Sir. It is Sunday evening."

The receptionist's voice held an apologetic note. All very well Guiseppe nattering on about playing cards, this was the President of the company and he expected the full treatment. It was a relief to see Andrew Merrin the General Manager walk into the foyer with the confident air of someone who had been in his job, and understood it well, for a very long time. Taking no chances, the mark of a good manager. He watched Merrin's thin lined face become younger as he smiled.

"Sir, how good to see you! We have been waiting for you; in fact, we had postponed dinner until your arrival. Mr Bertioni is so touched that you should have come all this way—as, of course, we all are. May I take your coat?"

Mr Jeudwine stubbed out his cigar in a glass ash tray, spilling ash on to the polished counter. Rubbish. Of course they hadn't waited, but it was a good line and this chap Merrin had been Manager for far too long now to quibble. And they wouldn't get another like him. Gentleman, dedicated, far too thin and exhausted looking, but that is what hotels are all about, he

11

thought, nodding at Merrin and allowing himself to be conducted to the lift with appropriate ceremony.

"I have brought Mr Vitold, my personal assistant," he said, watching the light as the lift descended. "I presume you have something for him?"

"Of course, Sir. I look forward to seeing him again."

Merrin had liked the good-looking Vitold, a protegé of Bertioni's, who had risen rather quickly from floor waiter to the banqueting department, and then to a spell on the reception desk before joining the Manager's office. Unlike Bertioni to have favourites, but Vitold was Polish, of good family, and had a definite presence; and there had been no higher rung up the ladder for him to climb while Andrew Merrin was General Manager, so it had been no surprise when, having made an impression on Mr Jeudwine too, he left to work for him in America.

But it had surprised and hurt Bertioni, who had taken Vitold's loyalty for granted!

"Chasing across the United States checking on the plumbing and how to cut costs and make profits, that is not the work of a hotelier," he had said to Andrew petulantly, lighting another cigarette and holding it elegantly between long fingers. "And Vitold could have been a good hotelier. I sometimes wonder if perhaps there is something else . . ."

Carrying the vicuna coat over his arm, Merrin waved the President ahead of him and pressed the button for the second floor.

"You know, I miss the old lift attendant," he said cheerfully, making conversation. "I like being greeted with a friendly 'good morning' or 'good evening'." Well, not always, he thought, smiling to himself and remembering old Arthur's wizened face and dislike of humanity, his sour comments on the world scene. Merrin had missed him when he retired. A mine of information, Arthur, knew everything that went on.

"That American senator in 435. Takes the lift up to the fourth floor and then walks down to the third. She's in 389—

12

wife of that newspaper proprietor. Can't fool me." Arthur's discretion lay in never mentioning names.

"Time and motion," replied Jeudwine sharply. He had observed Merrin's sudden smile and was irritated. "Can't afford to pay lift men to joy ride up and down all day or sit on their little stools reading the sporting pages. Being automatic has saved us thousands a year."

And that, thought Merrin, as he led the way out of the lift and along the gold-carpeted passage, is now our signature tune.

He opened the door with his pass key, lights full on inside, the heating turned up, a stylised arrangement of carnations and long-stemmed roses on the top of the television set.

God, how many times had he told them not to put flowers on the television. Moving the vase to a glass-topped table, he noticed the roses were not fresh; two sagged as if on broken necks, like pink cotton wool. That's what comes of having an outside shop to do the flowers. It would never have happened in Miss Ballater's day. Merrin broke off the heads of the two dead roses and dropped them in the waste-paper basket.

"Where is the drinks cupboard?" asked Jeudwine. He looked around the sitting room, standard lamps with parchment shades brought colour to light green walls, a discreetly chintzed sofa, mahogany writing desk and an easy chair upholstered in wine-coloured velvet. He had removed his jacket and Merrin noted the diamond pin which held his brightly-patterned tie, and the pearl buttons on the white silk shirt.

"We have not put them in the best suites, Sir," Merrin replied. "We felt that . . ." He hesitated, this was not going to be easy.

"You felt what?"

"We felt that our more important clients would prefer the personal service of a floor waiter rather than getting their own drinks out of a refrigerated cupboard."

It was a long sentence and Merrin could sense the President's impatience.

13

"And what about the time saved? The man power saved?"

"Well, we tried them out on other floors, and frankly . . ." Merrin floundered, his charming smile deserting him. "They have not been very popular. I think the laminated plastic looks out of place in these rooms, and the doors are not very well made—one fell off." He stopped suddenly, he was letting his feelings run away with him and this had been one of the President's own innovations. Hardly tactful, what was the matter with him tonight?

"They are here to stay," Mr Jeudwine said with finality. "And I want one in my room this evening. Now I must change. And, by the way," he stopped by the bedroom door, "it occurs to me that you have become a little out of date, Mr Merrin. Time moves on, you know."

The knock at the door, for which Merrin had been waiting, was discreet, but loud enough for Jeudwine to return.

"Come in," he called.

The waiter who entered carried a silver tray. On it was a bowl of olives and a glass of deep amber. Merrin looked quickly for the cherry, the frosted sugar round the rim of the glass. All was correct.

"Good evening, Sir. Your Manhatten."

Time moves on, thought Merrin, watching Jeudwine eat the cherry and drop the stick on the tray. You no longer have dark glossy hair, a fleshy olive skin and a bold eye for every teenage chambermaid, but you still like your Manhatten before dinner and you wouldn't have got that from your modern cupboard.

"Bring me another one while I have my tub," said Jeudwine, taking the glass and looking across at Merrin with eyes that narrowed but held a wry amusement. "O.K. Mr Merrin. I get your point. But I still want my drinks cupboard."

Vitold, having checked the luggage, looked round the Front Hall with pleasure. There was a hushed, almost claustrophobic atmosphere about a Sunday evening which he remembered well, and loved, for those had been the quiet hours on duty, quiet hours in which to let his mind wander and to dream. He had been a receptionist then, promoted from the banqueting department, and before that a floor waiter. Not a very enthusiastic one after five years in the army, and Bertioni had caught him drinking tea and smoking in the service kitchen while along the corridor the red light glowed unanswered. The reprimand had left him more unnerved than his first handling of a Bren gun. Later, Bertioni had returned to the service kitchen in softer mood, as if remembering the trainee who had been a relief waiter on the Manager's floor and who, after the fall of Warsaw, had left to join the Polish Army.

"Your parents had a hotel—you were going back there?" he had said to Vitold.

Bertioni's voice had been kind, and Vitold remembered the pale light from a window, high up and facing a brick wall, so that the rectangle of glass never came to life, and the way that light touched Bertioni's strong face, a face that had tightened, as if with anger, when Vitold had answered that he could not now go back. And he remembered, too, Bertioni's gentleness as he had turned to leave:

"I think we can arrange promotion for you, Vitold."

They had been good years behind the Reception desk, the camaraderie, the pride in work well done engendered by Bertioni, the careless laughter in the staff bar, and above all—Louise. The ice had begun to melt, there was to be another spring, life still left to be lived, if not in Poland, in a country no longer alien.

Vitold loitered purposefully, watching the two figures enter the lift. Was that Andrew Merrin? Vitold remembered his humorous advice when he worked under him as Assistant Manager. All the old faces, how would they be, and how would Louise be? He looked round the hall again, frowning. Something was missing from the enclosed world that had sheltered him for so long—it was the fragrance of flowers in the warm atmosphere, the awareness of roses, the heady challenge of dark carnations, a subtle sense of hidden gardens which had always pleased him. The flower arrangement at the foot of the curved staircase had great fronds of foliage and stiff tropical flowers that looked like birds but had no scent, and the flower kiosk by the side of the revolving doors had disappeared. In its place was a counter neat with brochures from travel agents and far-flung airlines. He had forgotten the new economy of Lincoln group to close the florist department and give the work to a nearby shop. The company accountants had been enthusiastic, but Vitold, to whom the vast stone and steel hotels which straddled America were faceless identikits, was saddened. The last flag of independence seemed to disappear with the loss of the flower counter and the pretty girl behind it. The Lincoln uniform of light blue suits worn through all the American hotels from page boy to general manager, had taken over like a tide of coloured emmets. But not at the Regina, thank God, thought Vitold, walking across the hall. The flowers might have gone, but not the Receptionist's dinner jacket.

"234 and 5, Sir. If we could have your name, please. Mr Jeudwine did not inform us, but of course your suite is waiting for you."

"Vitold. Spelt with a W but pronounced with a V. It is Polish. It is also my Christian name, one familiar in my country; but as my surname is very long and difficult to pronounce, I am known over here as Mr Vitold. I am also Mr Jeudwine's personal assistant. Does that help you?"

"Oh, yes, Sir, thank you—no one ever . . ."

"No one ever tells you anything?" Vitold interrupted with a smile. "They never do. I was a receptionist behind this same desk like you. I recall I was left on my own and had to receive Mr Jeudwine. I did not do very well." Here Vitold paused and looked at the young Receptionist with a gentle air, his dark eyes crinkled with a sudden humour.

"Indeed, I am very surprised that I am where I am now!" Vitold laughed. "You did very well. What is your name?"

"Crispin, Sir. I've filled in the form if you wouldn't mind signing, please. But, excuse me, if Mr Vitold is your surname, what initial should I put in front of it?"

"What indeed?" answered Vitold, looking at the confused young man on the other side of the counter. "What indeed?" he repeated in a quiet voice so full of sadness that Crispin looked away and began turning the pages of a ledger rather quickly, not seeing the neatly-written entries but thinking of his father's anger.

"Sold Poland up the river, our oldest allies," he would storm across the breakfast table; and Crispin, too young to have known the war himself, would understand that some reference to Yalta in *The Times* had sparked off further invective against the fur-hatted trio who had decided Poland's future.

Now the deep voice and far away look on the face of the ex-patriate Pole were echoes of past gallantry: pride, romantic encounters; and Crispin recalled with sudden clarity Sunday afternoons when his father's prized toy soldiers had been brought out as a childhood treat with battles fought and won on the dining room table.

"Try J, for Jan—that is what the President calls me."

Vitold hesitated for a moment, then added, "Give me a few moments. I won't keep you long."

Louise saw him standing just inside the door of the Banqueting Room, searching through the crowd with that eager but anxious look she knew so well. As she hurried towards him, the dark eyes caught hers. He smiled, waved, and was gone.

Adrian caught her arm.

"Louise, I've been looking for you. We must do something about ..."

"Later, there is someone I have to see ..."

The doorway was empty and she slipped through into the passage.

"Vitold!"

Against the clamour of waiters calling orders, the trolley wheels, clink of glasses, her voice was lost and the long passage was empty.

I should not have run to the door, I am too spontaneous, she thought, but seeing the well-loved figure so unexpectedly, deep eyes questing, Louise knew her instant reaction was one

17

of happiness and she always ran towards happiness. Vitold, here, tonight of all special nights, her friend and her lover for so many years.

"After all these years," Vitold would greet her on his rare visits, his voice still holding the faint accent she loved, his way of saying 'year', stretched out, slow, so that all the time was there.

"After all these years and it is still the same. You are still the same as that first day."

Vitold was no longer the shy, insecure waiter she had claimed, intrigued by his breeding, the shadows of a sad but romantic background. He was now an elegant hotelier, sure, competent. He had stood arrogantly in the doorway and raised a hand as if to say, "I am here," then disappeared.

Louise realised that, without thinking, she had run down the gold passage and now the solitary return seemed endless, the walls pressing in, like Alice in Wonderland, she thought, when she had eaten the wrong cakes. And there at the far end, Mr Garbin, the Banqueting Manager, was waiting for her.

"Lady Wearne, forgive me, but I need your help. There is a problem."

So many years—how many? Should she have gone and left it all; her father, Robin, the Regina, Adrian? Last of all, she realised, seeing Mr Garbin looking at her strangely, she had put Adrian.

"Yes, of course. What can I do?"

The smile, the charm, were so natural that Mr Garbin at once became voluble. He was a small man with bold appraising eyes that missed very little. When he was excited he used his hands, white and well cared for, to explain every point. Now they fluttered like doves.

"It's the cake, Lady Wearne. Monsieur Le Brun supervised the making of it himself and naturally he will present it, but he is an old man now and came in tonight just for the occasion . . . ."

His voice ran on. Had he seen her run along the passage, Louise wondered, angry with herself for feeling so concerned.

The years of training were still with her, her father's training.

"You must be beyond reproach," Bertioni had said when Adrian became Chairman, "like Caesar's wife—above suspicion."

"I thought Caesar's wife was supposed to be all things to all men," Louise had teased, and at her light, infectious laugh, Bertioni's severe face had softened.

"Louise, you are determined not to take anything seriously —irresistibly determined," he had added, looking at her affectionately.

Had she taken Vitold seriously? She remembered the first time she had been aware of him—on the towpath by the river. A Boat Race again after the war, and the crowds had relaxed in unexpectedly warm sunshine. Robin, her son, had rushed to look at a ginger cat sitting arrogantly in a cottage window and, leaning against some railings, she had allowed tears to fall unheeded in a sudden desperate despair for things as they were: her father's career, her marriage to Adrian ...

"Are you alright, Mrs Wearne?"

How angry she had been, brushing wet cheeks with the back of her hand, recognising a member of the Regina staff. And how angry Bertioni would have been.

"Never let your private life be known by the staff."

So many times he had said this, with that arrogant tilt of his head which Louise loved. "Always," he would continue, "they must look up to you, respect you, fear you a little as someone to admire and to follow, but never, never to be understood."

Vitold had bought her brandy in the pub nearby, sitting in the half light beneath windows still fitted with cardboard after the last bomb had shattered the glass. The strong shoulders under the tweed jacket, thick brown hair and deep watchful eyes had attracted her at once, and she had become light-hearted again and asked him back to tea. How patient he had been with Robin, telling him the story of the bear cub adopted by the Polish Army, how it was called Voytek and grew to be six foot tall and carried the ammunition. She had used Voytek as an excuse and asked Vitold to come with her and buy a teddy bear for Robin. They had spent the day together, but it was not until that rainy afternoon of Victory day that they had first loved each other. How wet she had been; then the hot steamy bath and cuddling beside him under rough blankets. Dear Vitold, dear, very dear Vitold . . .

"So you see, my lady, the problem."

Garbin had come to a halt and was looking at her, shoulders hunched, hands turned palms uppermost, seeking an answer.

Louise came slowly back—something to do with the cake and the old chef, Monsieur Le Brun and a long evening. She was filled with such happiness and longing that she was afraid the glow she felt must be visible.

"I understand." Louise, concentrating, gave her brightest smile. "I will go down and see him."

Garbin watched her admiringly, like an excited thorough-bred leaping unknown fences, she was away. Hurrying to keep up with her, he reached the swing doors to the kitchens and held one steady.

"Oh, I love coming down here. All the delicious sniffs and the bustle . . . " Louise, quite unaware of the distraction caused by her fair hair and the elegance of her dress, smiled at an astonished commis stirring a vast copper pan.

"And there is my dear Monsieur Le Brun," she said, as a white-clad figure emerged from an inner office, the round moon face alight with pleasure.

"*Comment ça va, mon ami?*"

THREE

Mr Bertioni was feeling happy. So many old friends, so many warm handshakes, it was as if the whole of his life at the Regina had been spanned in this past half hour. He had greeted the last of the line, when he saw Robert Jeudwine make an unhurried entrance, wearing a large blue velvet bow-tie with his dinner jacket, and carrying a small package.

"Carlo, my felicitations! I hope I haven't been holding up the proceedings?"

He patted Bertioni's arm. "A small present from Tiffany's —no, don't open it now, let's eat first. I'm starved."

Bertioni looked round, saw Garbin, the Banqueting Manager watching him, and nodded.

Three sharp raps of the gavel, the conversation falling away, a sudden laugh, clink of glasses, then silence.

"Ladies and gentlemen, dinner is served."

Bertioni led the way through an arch into the dining room beyond, pinkly lit with the long head table on a dais facing the room.

"I hope I'm sitting next to your beautiful daughter," said Jeudwine, threading his way through small round tables, silver and glass gleaming on starched white cloths, small bowls of anemones, scarlet and purple clusters of colour. He noticed the slivers of butter on ice, the stuffed avocado pears, the plates of curved Melba toast, and felt soothed. The Hotel Regina was an old-fashioned hotel by the Lincoln standards, but he had to admit it had a style they never achieved.

"She insisted," answered Bertioni, smiling. He liked the tough little American, admired his astuteness, and was touched by the use of his Christian name, Carlo. In all the years at the Regina, no one had reached that familiarity, not even Sir John Worsfield. Bertioni put his hand in his pocket to stroke the silver cigarette case given to him by the old Chairman so many years ago. It was a familiar gesture performed many times a day. The case, smoothly warm beneath his touch, never failed to bring back a little of the magic of that May evening in 1945. It had begun badly with Ernest, Sir John's old waiter, refusing to accept a glass of champagne to celebrate the end of the war.

"I shall keep the cork, Sir John. I would prefer that."

He had retired, flushed, but with dignity, carrying his silver tray, and the Chairman had been rueful.

"Meant well. We've been together through two wars now. I just wanted to share it with him."

Sitting in his high-backed chair in front of a coal fire, the Chairman had looked strangely forlorn. The furnishings of his sitting room were forlorn too, plain, austere, in safe muted shades.

"Ernest doesn't like change," Bertioni had explained, wanting to comfort.

He remembered that the Chairman had talked about change at some length, how much more difficult it would be to run the Regina without the challenge of a war which made discipline and keeping up standards a battle cry.

"Now it's all over and the reins have gone slack—I don't envy you the next decade, Mr Bertioni."

He had held out his glass for more champagne, and it was then that they had disagreed. Even now Bertioni could not remember what it had been about, except that it had been an idea of Adrian's, which Sir John had put forward, and Bertioni had been touchy, as he always was, knowing Sir John's nephew would one day become Chairman, and he would have his son-in-law as his boss.

Depressed, Bertioni had stood up to leave, and the Chairman had stopped him.

"This was meant to be a celebration. I may not say very

much about it, but I am very much aware of all your efforts and great loyalty."

The silver cigarette case he had handed Bertioni was engraved inside the lid in his own handwriting:

TO CARLO BERTIONI
IN APPRECIATION
JOHN WORSFIELD.

The emotion that swept over Bertioni then had not smudged with the years. It was as deep and moving now as on that spring evening when it had brought tears to his eyes, tears which had embarrassed the Chairman. He remembered how he had passed the lift and walked down the stairs from the Chairman's top floor suite in order to prolong that moment of utter happiness, singing softly as he went Puccini's song of the shepherd boy, the clear dawn song which never failed to arouse in him a feeling of new beginnings, the promise of excitements to come.

Now he placed the small blue box with its black lettering TIFFANY AND CO on the table in front of him, and saw for the first time the Victorian posy of Parma violets beside his plate. The Regina colour, he thought, picking up the tiny envelope. On the card inside was written:

HAPPY BIRTHDAY. WITH ADMIRATION AND
AFFECTION, ROWENNA BALLATER.

So that was what the R stood for. All these years he had wondered about the private life of the severe manager of the florists department. She had the strong, rather harsh good looks of an Italian peasant, he thought, looking down and seeing her settling herself at one of the round tables with Moxon and Pierre, the old Banqueting Manager. Very handsome, in her Regina purple dress; and her hair, now grey, carefully curled. Catching his eye, she smiled, rather shyly, and Bertioni picked up the violets and gave a small bow. He had a sudden wish to blow her a kiss, a wish he quickly restrained. Miss Ballater was devoted to the order of things, the rightness of behaviour, which was why she had been such an admirable member of the staff, and she would have been dismayed by such familiarity on his behalf. All the same, he thought, putting the posy beside the Tiffany box, I think I should have done it, I'm very touched by her.

"What has happened to Louise?" Beryl Bertioni's voice was sharp rather than anxious. Sitting on her husband's right, she was fiddling with the clasp of her evening bag.

"Don't put on your glasses," Bertioni said quickly, sensing her purpose, "you look so charming without them. And Louise will be here soon."

As he spoke, Bertioni saw his daughter arrive, and, as always, he knew that surge of love as the slim, blue-clad figure made her way towards the top table. A new dress, soft floating material and her hair fluffed into a pale gold frame round the bright animated face. She paused several times to greet old members of the staff, their eyes following her after she had passed. She can't help creating an entrance, thought Bertioni fondly, waiting for her. A breath of Arpege told him she was there as she stopped behind him and bent to kiss the top of his head.

"I've just been down to the kitchens to see Monsieur Le Brun," said Louise, "and he's not coming up for dinner, prefers to make his entrance with the cake, bless him. So will I have an empty place beside me?"

"No," replied Bertioni quickly, aware that all the tables were filled and there must be no waiting. "The President has brought Vitold and he will be sitting next to you."

Three sharp taps again with the gavel from Mr Garbin, then Bertioni surprised everyone. Standing up, he said in his strong voice:

"For what the Lord has given us, may we be truly thankful."

"You've never said Grace before," said Beryl, settling herself like an elderly poodle in its basket.

"I've a lot to be thankful for," replied Bertioni, patting the plump little hand now unfolding a snowy napkin. "And so have you. So let's enjoy ourselves. Talk to Mr Jeudwine, he's

24

only just arrived and has flown over specially from the States for my birthday."

He listened to the rise and fall of voices, at first subdued, now growing stronger, like birds chattering in the eaves. A waiter appeared at his side, poured two golden inches into his long-stemmed wine glass, and Bertioni sipped. *Montrachet*, chilled like a mountain stream. He nodded approval.

"Happy birthday," said the voice on his left, and Bertioni turned, smiling, to Charlotte Merrin.

"I've neglected you, my dear. Forgive me, but I must tell you that it was my special request to have you next to me."

Not quite true, he sipped his wine and raised his glass.

"To you, Mrs Merrin—no, tonight I shall call you Charlotte."

"We haven't enough women at the top table," Louise had lamented. "There's only me and mother, and we can't have a row of penguins facing everybody."

She had been sitting on the edge of his desk, laughing, swinging long slim legs in Rayne shoes.

"Adrian thought if we had one head of a department we would have to have them all, so it's just dear old Monsieur Le Brun and the Manager and his wife," she stopped suddenly, grinning impishly. "Of course, Charlotte! She can sit next to you. You always rather fancied her, didn't you?"

Bertioni smiled back. "Perhaps. Years ago she was my secretary with a trim little figure and pretty legs. Now she is rather a plump little pigeon; but, yes, I would like to have her next to me."

"She's still got nice hair and skin and lovely eyes," said Louise loyally, "and pretty legs too if you bothered to look."

"First you wear long skirts down to you ankles so that one can't see," replied Bertioni amiably, lighting a cigarette, "and then you have them up to your navel so that one daren't see."

Louise put back her head and laughed happily. It wasn't often that her father joked, and never about women, like

25

whistling in a cathedral. She had swung her legs and jumped down from the desk.

"Poor Charlotte," she said, "she only put on weight out of boredom."

"You never do," said Bertioni fondly, inhaling and letting the smoke drift through half-closed lips.

"I'm never bored," said Louise, planting a kiss on the top of his head. "And you smoke too much."

"Far away?" asked the soft voice beside him. "You haven't eaten your avocado or opened your present."

"Forgive me." Bertioni raised his glass. "Which shall I do first?"

How good looking he still was, thought Charlotte; and always would be with those finely planed cheek bones and eloquent dark eyes.

"The avocado, I think," she replied. "It is filled with all sorts of delicacies, then you will have plenty of time to open your box. How exciting. I've never had anything from Tiffany's."

"How's things?" asked Adrian on her left.

"Fine." Charlotte could never think of anything to say to Adrian. She sometimes wondered if he remembered that evening during the war when he had taken her to dinner at the Dorchester, their first date together and their last. Conversation had dwindled and a curious lethargy had settled over their table while the electric organ beat out "I haven't time to be a millionaire" and dancing couples laughed and sang to each other. It was then that Louise had arrived at their table. Dining alone with her father, she had seen them from the other side of the room and Charlotte had introduced them, watching Adrian become alive and as carefree as the bright vision before him. They had danced away together, and Charlotte had found herself sitting with Bertioni. It was the only comfortable time in the whole evening, she remembered. Bertioni had asked her opinion of the new organ, now blaring away "Music, Maestro, please", and she had said it reminded her of a fairground. They had both decided it was not for the Regina and drank Hock together and she had been happy and relaxed. And here she was, all these years later, sitting between the two of them, feeling as awkward with Adrian as ever. She glanced at Bertioni and he looked up and smiled.

"You're looking very charming," he said. "I like that Edwardian blouse with all its ruffles."

He picked up the blue box in front of him. "What do you think is in it?" he asked. "Guess."

Charlotte shook her head. "I can't think, unless perhaps it is a cigarette lighter."

"Beryl," said Bertioni, touching his wife's arm, "tell Mr Jeudwine I am about to open his present, the mystery is to be solved."

How happy he is, thought Charlotte, he has an almost boyish air as if everything is spread out before him. She watched the long tapered fingers open the box. Inside was a round paper weight made of crystal. Bertioni held it in the palm of his hand.

"I like the feel of it," he said.

Jeudwine leaned forward across Beryl and called:

"Hold it up to the light."

Bertioni did so, twirling the circle of glass from side to side.

"Ah," he said, with great satisfaction, "how splendid, how really splendid. See Beryl," he turned to her, "inside there is written HOTEL REGINA."

"I can't see without my glasses," she grumbled, fumbling for the purse on her lap.

Bertioni looked over the bent grey head, chrysanthemum curled, and saluted the President with a wave of his hand.

"This will be treasured," he said. "Thank you a thousand times."

"What are they all looking at?" asked Mrs Lobb. She had turned to stare at the top table as something was being passed from one side of Bertioni to the other.

"A present, I expect," Lobb answered. He was looking at the plate which had just been placed before him and dabbling at the creamy sauce with his fork.

27

Pierre, who had been watching the top table, also turned his attention to the plate before him.

"Quenelles," he said with authority. "Salmon, I have no doubt. One of Mr Bertioni's favourites."

Miss Ballater gave a quick little smile to Moxon and picked up the menu.

"I expect it's all here," she said, "and how nice to give us a menu each so that we can keep them."

She looked across at Mrs Lobb, whose kind eyes in a thin pale face now held an expression of anxiety. Her darkly dyed hair had been freshly waved and she wore a green velvet dress with a lace collar.

"I never quite know what quenelles are," said Miss Ballater, taking a small mouthful, "but they're absolutely delicious. Do tell us, Mr Pierre, you're the expert."

The ex-Banqueting Manager put down his fork. "First prepare salmon Mousseline," he said pontifically. He was aware that he had an audience, even Lobb had put aside the notes he had been making for his speech, to look at him with interest.

"What's this mousse business?" he asked.

Moxon laughed. "Prefer fish and chips, eh Norman?"

"Mousseline," repeated Pierre, not to be deterred, "is minced salmon, boned and skinned, mixed well in a bowl with egg whites, then you pass it through a sieve and stir in cream." He paused. Mrs Lobb was looking at him in a bemused way, fork poised half way to her mouth.

"Then you shape the Mousseline into small ovals and poach them in boiling salted water for about ten minutes . . ."

"Like poached eggs?" queried Mrs Lobb cheerfully, interrupting. "Poached eggs on haddock, that's our favourite, though poaching eggs isn't all that easy. Do you just drop yours into a pan or do you have those little plastic cup things?" she asked Miss Ballater.

"Ted used to like a poached egg," she went on without waiting for a reply. "Nice thick piece of toast and plenty of butter. Always gave him a cooked breakfast and cleaned his shoes till they shone. Do the same with Norman, look after him, though he's retired."

Moxon, watching Miss Ballater confess in a charming way that she could not even boil an egg, saw little Mrs Friggens was now at ease. Mrs Friggens? Goodness, that was going back a bit, when she had been married to Ted Friggens, the Chief Engineer. Good chap, Ted, knew his job. They'd had some companionable drinks in the staff bar, Guinness with a Rum for Ted. Little chap with dog-like brown eyes, trusting, always quoting Churchill.

"Well, here's to the task and the toil," he would say, raising his glass.

And Lobb, big lumbering Lobb, twice his size, would sigh and correct him:

"Come then let us to the task and the toil . . ."

It was Lobb who had found Ted, still clutching his dog, both dead, entombed in the rubble of his house in the cupboard under the stairs.

Mrs Friggens—Moxon never could remember her name. Of course, Hilda. Friggens used to say, looking down at his feet, "My Hilda wouldn't let me be seen dead without my shoes polished."

Moxon had a sudden thought of those shoes, flattened out of shape, battered from leather into crumbled brick dust.

"Well, boiling an egg's not that easy either."

Flushed and confident now, Mrs Lobb was leaning across a silent Pierre.

"Of course Norman's on a diet now—doctor's orders." She had a high rather whining voice which it was impossible to ignore.

Moxon gave a sympathetic smile to Pierre, who had been silenced in mid sentence. "And what's to come?" he asked.

"Saddle of lamb, pommes Anna, braised celery . . ."

"And roast potatoes, I hope," said Lobb, "no diet tonight."

"And," continued Pierre, not to be stopped in full flow this time, "a very pleasant Margaux."

Moxon, looking across the table, remembered it all.

29

Hilda Friggens. She had been on her weekly visit to her mother and returned to find she had lost home, husband and a much-loved dog. All her life had been spent caring and now suddenly in one stroke there was no one and no home to cherish. It was Bertioni who had offered her a job as house-keeper.

"Said he needed her," confided Lobb over his gin in the staff bar, "needed her help to show how to run a home properly, which is what the Regina is all about. It's made all the difference to her, I tell you I've been quite worried. It's not just losing Ted, it's losing someone to care for."

"Better let her look after you," Moxon had said with a smile, ordering the other half. "You're both lonely since your Mary's gone and I reckon Ted would be pleased."

"Funny thing," said Lobb, bringing Moxon back to the present and signalling to a waiter to refill their glasses, "but writing this speech I keep going back to the war days, there was such a good feeling about then. It was never quite the same after we pushed out Churchill."

"We got him back later."

"Yes, but he was tired then, run out of wham, as most of us had."

"You didn't run out of wham when Mr Jeudwine bought that new carpet for the Coronation! Never heard you go on so."

"Yes, nearly got me the sack that did," Lobb said.

"Bertioni was on my side, of course, but as he said, 'orders are orders and the chain of authority must not be broken.' Then he added with one of those looks of his which are meant to be a smile, 'but they can be bent sometimes'."

Moxon laughed. "I always remember the day your lot from the Works Department laid that carpet in the Front Hall. Red, white and blue, sort of jazzy—bloody awful. Then when they stripped the gold carpet off the staircase and started putting it up there, well, you just disappeared."

"Saw Miss Ballater's face—frozen with horror she was."

"What was I frozen about?" Glad to get away from Mrs

Lobb's domestic monologue and feeling she had done her bit, Miss Ballater turned gratefully to Moxon.

"We were talking about the Coronation carpet," said Moxon, "and you looking horrified."

"Well, so I was. Imagine having to arrange flowers to go with that. In the end I just did great bowls of white lilac."

Moxon remembered the soft fragrance when he'd arrived in the early morning. Later it had been submerged in the usual drift of scents and cigar smoke that wafted through the Front Hall as it came to life, every room in the hotel full and still more hopefuls with their bright new luggage arriving in rain-streaked taxis.

"Never known so many Americans in the Regina," he was drinking his morning pint with Miss Ballater, "and one blue-haired matron from California thought the carpet was just dandy, so patriotic. Which was, I suppose, what Mr Jeudwine had in mind."

"It put paid to my Arum lilies, though," Miss Ballater had sighed. "The stamens would have looked so wonderful against the old gold carpet." She finished her glass. "Why don't you have something warmer to celebrate, it's to chilly today? Let me buy you one for once." She had a shy smile.

"No, not even this once." Moxon smiled back, knowing she would understand. This was his male stronghold. As head of the Florist's Department, he had no doubt Miss Ballater earned more than he did, but in his book a man was boss and Moxon intended it to stay that way.

"This will have to be a quick one." He had brought back another gin and tonic and a large whisky for himself, "have some new chaps and they keep disappearing to watch the television. Can't blame them, I suppose. There wasn't a single pageboy either half an hour ago."

They drank to the Queen—"and to Everest," he remembered lifting his glass again. "And to you," he had added, greatly daring, "you are looking very nice."

He remembered the dark blue suit and the white blouse with a red pattern, and how she had drained her glass and stood up abruptly. Afraid of compliments, he thought, must be careful.

"Did you see the rainbow?" he asked as he held open the pub door.

"Yes, it seemed to arch from the Palace to Westminster Abbey and everyone cheered. They didn't seem to mind the cold. I had my top coat on and I was frozen coming here this morning." Miss Ballater shivered and prepared to hurry down the wet pavement to the Regina.

"Well, put your top coat on again this evening. I know a nice pub by the river and we can watch fireworks."

For a moment he thought he had gone too far, the dark blue shoulders turned from him seemed to stiffen, then, quickly she had turned round, inhibitions forgotten, for once spontaneous.

"Oh, wouldn't that be fun!" He had never heard her so responsive, almost girlish.

Coronation day, years gone, but how clear every moment—remembered.

Moxon looked across at Miss Ballater now, grey-haired, elegant in her purple dress, wondered a little, and knew it could never have been.

"Great pity sex was ever invented," his father in his wheel chair in the Star and Garter Home garden, a rug over his knees that had no legs beneath them.

"Well, what about me then?" Moxon had laughed and filled their glasses with the Guinness he had brought. "Where would I be?"

He remembered a blackbird singing in its clear loud voice, bright beak open, happy with his world and happy to sing about it on the top of a flowering cherry tree.

His father had ignored his remark, brushed his moustache and then his nose with the same arch of the back of his hand.

"Look at me now. Can't do anything any more so I don't have to worry. I just have friends, like the lady who comes with the books. If I give her a box of chocolates and we do the crossword together, she isn't thinking what I am up to, because she knows I can't be up to anything and so we enjoy that half hour. I look forward to it all the week and she always arrives looking as if she does too, bless her."

Moxon recalled his father's funeral, the old comrades still left were there in their fawn raincoats and bowler hats, carefully polished shoes and the only colour the lines of ribbon worn with pride. Among the wreaths outside the crematorium had been a bunch of yellow roses. "From the Book Lady", he'd read, "remembering many happy hours."

There was no middle-aged lady in sensible shoes as Moxon had expected, no stranger at all, except a girlish figure in a bright blue coat with springy, reddish hair and a freckled nose. She had looked at him hesitantly, then turned and walked away down the asphalt path.

"Wake up," said Miss Ballater, touching his hand.

"I was thinking of the fireworks in that pub by the river on Coronation night," smiled Moxon.

A waiter was placing a plate of roast lamb before him, another served a silver dish of vegetables by his left side. Temporarily diverted, Moxon's preoccupation went unnoticed. He sipped his claret, which Pierre had insisted on sampling first, head on one side, before giving considered approval. Moxon sipped again and the red-haired girl had disappeared.

"Well, it didn't last long," said Pierre.

"What?" asked Moxon, helping himself to mint sauce.

"The carpet, of course."

"Oh, we're back to that."

"Haven't left it," said Mrs Friggens, "never saw it myself, of course, up on the floors."

"Two weeks, that's all," said Lobb, "and I had the devil's own job getting the old carpet back in time. Just took it for granted when Bertioni said 'have it cleaned' that it would be done before he could turn round." He paused to taste his red wine.

"Very nice, Pierre, I agree with you. I might have known he was up to something when he said about bending the line of authority, or something like that—not like Bertioni. I've always wanted to know how he managed it."

Miss Ballater touched Moxon's arm.

"Shall I tell them?" she asked.

"Why not," he smiled.

"I was doing the flowers at the bottom of the stairs early one morning," she began, "when I was aware of a presence at the top, looking down as he always did, but this time with an expression of such distaste on his face that I thought I'd done something wrong. Anyway, he came down and said to me:

"'What would happen if you upset some water on that carpet?'

"'I never upset water,' I replied."

Moxon, who had been watching from his corner, grinned now as he remembered her asperity.

"Then, he said: 'Well, supposing you were to spill a little and the colours were to run, we wouldn't be able to use the carpet, would we?'"

"I remember the stain on that carpet," said Lobb; "looked more like red ink to me."

Miss Ballater looked at Moxon and they both laughed.

"It was," she said.

"Had to help things along a little," said Moxon, "and I just happened to have a bottle in my cubby hole. The thing was, the damn carpet *was* waterproof!"

As their laughter rose, Bertioni looked down, then turned to Charlotte:

"I wonder what has amused them so much?"

"Reminiscing, I expect. They are all old friends happy to be together."

"Yes, we're all happy to be together tonight," said Bertioni, raising his glass and smiling at Charlotte. "I must have a birthday more often."

FOUR

Louise was so aware of the empty place beside her, waiting, knowing why Vitold was late, that she trembled, her hand knocking the glass of wine, runaway rivulets chasing across the white cloth. At once, a flurry of waiters, a clean napkin placed over the offending stain, and Jeudwine turned, smiling sympathetically and even more grateful at being released from Mrs Bertioni's monologue.

"Good evening, beautiful Louise. How are you?"

"Beautiful," Louise laughed back, "but careless. I have just knocked over my wine."

"Mind not on the job?"

Little Jewish tycoon, old body, young desires—don't come too near. No, my mind is not on the job but it is not for you to say or know.

"Well you've let the side down too tonight," she said pertly.

"How?" Jeudwine's voice was abrupt, the teasing intimacy faded a little.

Unperturbed, Louise reached for her evening bag.

"You haven't got your usual button hole," she said, "but not to worry, I have one for you." She produced a carefully wrapped clove carnation, held it to her nose and smiled.

"It even has a scent," she smiled, placing it beside Jeudwine's plate.

"For our President, with my love."

Jeudwine was touched, though a faint suspicion remained to ruffle him. Then, looking at the bright face beside him framed in scented hair, he relaxed.

"How good of you, my dear." He fussed with the lapel of his jacket. "Wish you could fix it for me."

"Can't reach, alas. But you've done it beautifully. Now you look perfect."

Louise regarded him with her head on one side.

"Yes, all's well with the world now—the Regina world, that is."

"How did you know I wouldn't have a carnation?" asked Jeudwine, turning his attention to his plate, cutting a portion, putting his knife to one side, and spearing it with his fork.

"You couldn't very well," replied Louise amiably, "the shop that does the flowers now closes at lunch time on Saturdays, and doesn't open again until tomorrow."

Jeudwine was silent.

"So," continued Louise, "I cossetted this in a cool place for nearly two days."

She sang the word 'cossetted', looking sideways at him in a way Jeudwine found provocative, knowing it was meant to be and not minding. He felt rather strong and male beside her.

Louise raised her glass.

"You know you should bring back the Florist's Department and the kiosk in the Front Hall—the Regina isn't the same without it."

"It's not meant to be the same. Times change and its cheaper to have a franchise."

Jeudwine did not want to talk hotel politics with this girl who excited him, he preferred her frivolous banter and fell silent.

"But it's not cheaper," persisted Louise. "You have to pay for the franchise, and girls from the Florist's Department would run the kiosk as part of their job—and look much more decorative," she added.

Jeudwine did not reply and Louise, after a small pause, spoke hurriedly, her voice rather high.

"I suppose you think the Regina is old fashioned? Well, it

is," she answered herself. "That's what you should capitalise on—our old-fashionedness and love of service."

Louise had been aware during the last minute that Vitold had slipped in to the seat beside her and now she felt his hand on her knee.

"Good evening," said Vitold, claiming her attention, "we haven't had a chance to speak. You look enchanting, as always." His eyes were amused, but held warning lights. You are going too far, you are over pitched, a little my fault, perhaps. Louise saw his tender smile and knew he was thinking—he had said it to her so often—"You are always over excited when you are fighting your father's battles". It was all there in his anxious eyes, in the protective touch of his hand. Don't rush your fences. Calm down.

"Lady Wearne has got a lot to say to the President."

Mrs Lobb, cheeks now taking on a pinker hue, chewed her way through another roast potato, then washed it down with a gulp of claret, leaving powdery fragments on the rim of her glass. She was enjoying herself.

"Looked as if she was laying into him, if you ask me, waving her hands about proper. Quietened down a bit since that chap came beside her. Bit late, wasn't he—expect they will have kept something hot for him. Don't recognise him myself."

Lobb, seeing his glass had been replenished, did not reply, but thumbed through his notes and sat silently. Miss Ballater was talking to Moxon quietly, almost shyly. Observing them, Pierre turned to Mrs Lobb.

"You've got the best view but you mustn't stare too much," he scolded, "It's a party, after all, and they wouldn't like it."

All the same, Pierre shifted his shoulders round in as laconic a fashion as he could manage.

"Oh," he said delighted to be in the know. "That is Mr Vitold. Before your time, perhaps. Real gentleman, Polish, and Mr Bertioni thought highly of him. Started as a floor waiter, then joined up. When he came back he went in

Reception. Your Ted would have known him. I had him for a while in Banqueting. Going places, he was, then Mr Jeudwine snaffled him as his personal assistant. Couldn't very well refuse, I suppose. All the same, I was suprised he left the Regina with Bertioni backing him like that and everything going for him."

Waiters were active removing plates, placing clean napkins over wine stains.

"Is this the cake?" asked Mrs Lobb. She produced a compact from her bag and patted vigorously at her pink reflection. There was the tired scent, sickly, of old powder.

Louise felt a quietness that isolated her from the rise and fall of voices, laughter, clink of glasses, the discreet clatter as plates were removed and her father's favourite mint ice-cream, pale green in silver goblets, took their place. Elaborate baskets of *friandises*, carved from spun sugar, were carried with ceremony to each table, and there were exclamations of pleasure and the sounds rose, enveloping her ...

Years ago. How many years ago in that hot summer after the war? They still lived at Richmond then and she had gone to Kew with Vitold on one of his days off, wandering along the river bank, hand in hand, anonymous, at peaceful ease with one another.

"It would be a happy thing, *moja kochana*," Vitold had said, using a Polish endearment, "if round that next bend where the ducks are floating on the water, there should be a little inn with white chairs and tables set outside, and a high cuisine," He'd stopped and kissed her cheek. There was the faint gurgle of the river water sucking at the grass bank. The ground was dry beneath clumps of cow-parsley and cracked into strange shapes.

"And," he'd continued, "I should buy it at once and we would set up house together and I would cook and you would serve in a Polish peasant dress and looking so beautiful that the people would come from all the corners of the world."

Laughing, Louise had started to run, pulling Vitold, the sun against her back.

38

"If it is there it is a sign and we will run away and be happy for ever."

No inn had appeared round the corner, no dwelling at all, just the pollarded willows and the water creases behind two gliding swans. They had sat down on the dusty verge.

"I had a mare once at home," Vitold had said, staring across the river. "Wilful, she rushed her fences. I fell so many, many times. My father was angry—always I had bruises, limping."

"'She must go,' he'd said. 'You do not train her. Always you let her take you—you should take her.'"

Vitold had reached to take Louise's hand.

"My father, he did not understand. I liked her to rush fences, I liked her spirit of abandon. But then one day she did too much, I could not hold her and there was foam on her nostrils and on her neck and I knew then that I had failed her, I had let her go too far and now I had left it too late to change her. So, you see, *moja kochana*, how I love your spirit and the way you leap over every obstacle, and I would like to say leap with me and leave your life and come away and have my love, always and always, and then I remember that it is not kind to let all that spirit to go unchecked and I must remind you of your husband and son and your duty to them."

Louise remembered her reply: "Perhaps they would not be too unhappy." And Vitold had sighed, his dark eyes very sad.

"You say that in the carefree sunlit way which is yours alone, but now I check you as you are about to leap into love and life with me and I say, 'What of your father?' and I know without looking at you that a distressed and serious cloud has crossed your face, for the one fence you would not leap is the one that would separate you from your father."

"You make it sound like incest."

"Perhaps, in a way. If I lived up to him in your mind you would come away with me and it would be a peace and a haven and a love for ever—for me. But for you—you would be happy for a little while and then that little shadow would become a man—a tall man with a chiselled, handsome face, arrogant, demanding, your whole world, and you would go back. This, I think, *moja kochana*, is the saddest, most profound moment of my life, for I have to say I love him a little too."

Louise sat very still in her chair at the top table, her hands clasped between her knees like a small girl. She could feel again the warm sun and see, along the river's edge, the curious patterns that had formed in the baked mud. She had traced them, as she listened to Vitold, with an invisible finger, her mind on the shapes, so that his words would not consume her totally. She had not wanted to be consumed. She had not wanted to come to a decision. She had wanted it to go on forever as it was—Vitold working at the Regina with a day off during the week, a day they could plan together.

They had returned to London with dark clouds bruising the sky and running up the steps to Vitold's flat they had been caught in sudden torrential rain, while he fumbled for the key. They had laughed and dried each other and loved and drunk vodka—oh, blissful day and she had thrown it all away. A month later Vitold had accepted Jeudwine's offer to become his Personal Assistant in America. Jeudwine—she remembered the desolation which had overwhelmed her—

Then, she took a deep breath and turned to talk to him.

"You've been very quiet," he said. "Jan not looking after you?"

"Jan?" for a moment she was puzzled, then smiled. "Oh, Vitold—he's deep in conversation with the waiter who has been serving him. They once worked together so he is very happy gossiping as all hotel people do."

"Everyone talks shop," replied Jeudwine, "it's just that the shops are different."

He turned to answer Mrs Bertioni, who had put her hand on his arm to claim his attention, and Louise looked quickly at Vitold.

"Am I going to see you properly?" she whispered.

Vitold put his knife and fork together and signalled for the waiter to remove his plate.

"Ah, now I have caught up," he lifted his glass to her.

"And what is properly?" he asked, laughing.

Louise knew she was blushing.

"After all these years," Vitold's eyes changed from amusement to tenderness, "you blush like a girl. I find that very . ."

"This is very good ice-cream," Jeudwine interrupted, and Louise turned quickly from Vitold, who was teasing and exciting her and she knew her cheeks were still flushed.

"For an American that's very high praise," she smiled.

"I thought you were going to say that naturally it is good if it was made in the Regina kitchens—or something of that kind."

"I nearly did," confessed Louise, "but . . . " I was overdoing it before, she thought, knowing that Vitold was listening beside her.

"But," Jeudwine pounced. "But you thought I had heard enough about the Regina for one evening? On the contrary, I rather enjoy your enthusiasm and loyalty and, tomorrow morning, if it will make you happy, I shall have a session with your father—it will stop me having to go and visit my niece with your mother!"

The last part of his sentence came in a conspiritorial whisper and Louise laughed.

"Well, Patsy has only had her appendix out, and in great luxury, so not to worry, but a visit to the bedside with mother, who revels in hospital details, poor you. Anything is better than that—even a flower kiosk," she added mischievously.

Jeudwine looked at her in admiration.

"It's quite absurd to think of you as Robin's mother."

"Then don't, please," answered Louise quickly. "I don't. I don't think of time at all otherwise it is so depressing and we are so obsessed with age in this country. Forty-year-old

41

matron slips on a banana skin. Ridiculous, what has age got to do with it? At forty she could have three lovers!"

And I wonder how many you have? Jeudwine looked at her appraisingly, admiring her animation.

"The young are so serious these days," he said, "they don't seem to enjoy themselves in the carefree way we did. And still can," he added, looking at Louise with bold, questioning eyes.

"And do." Louise looked ahead to avoid his closeness. "I find life is wonderful as long as you just let it happen and don't get too technical."

Vitold was silent beside her, she did not like him in this teasing, provocative mood and continued her conversation with Jeudwine.

"Take your niece Patsy," she said. "When she came over to write that 'Swinging London' article, and Robin used to take her out, she would sit in the restaurants with a notebook and work out how many pseudo intellectuals, jobless, drop-outs or what have you were there, and whether it was because of life's deprivation, fear of the bomb or dissatisfaction with the government." Louise laughed. "I ask you! She should have been dancing the night away and left them to it. People were there because they wanted to be there. No other reason. Simple as that."

"You would have danced the night away?" asked Jeudwine. He had a sudden recollection of dancing with her years ago, light and scented and looking up at him through that cloud of hair as if no one else mattered. He had ended the dance promising to make her father Managing Director.

"Of course," Louise laughed. "Anyway, serious or not, Patsy is exactly right for Robin. She's so much brainier, and he finds that very impressive, which is good for him."

Louise looked sideways at him. "Do you realise that we are almost related?" she asked wickedly. "Your niece married to my son—let's work that one out."

They discussed it animatedly, asking Vitold's opinion. Then Louise sighed.

42

"All the same, it's a bit depressing to think of Robin as married, though why I should say that of someone old enough to have served in Northern Ireland ..." Her voice trailed away, then she turned to Vitold with her old gaiety.

"I liked it best when you told him the story of Voytek and helped me buy a teddy bear for him. Do you remember?"

Now she's teasing *me* ... Vitold, looking at her bright face, wide mouth parted a little, watched her lick her lips with the tip of her tongue.

"I remember," replied Vitold gravely. But it wasn't then we became lovers, he reflected. My fault. I was too inhibited, the Polish waiter with no homeland and the flower-like girl married to the Regina's Chairman.

Below them, Tom Raffin, the Publicity Director, was arranging two arc lights to face the door. Aided by the Head Electrician, he switched them on and off with assurance, a man of authority in his well-cut dinner jacket.

"Tom Raffin is looking very sleek," said Vitold, following her gaze, "Does he still live with you?"

"He is supposed to be getting married," said Louise, by way of an answer.

"Married? That will please you, perhaps?"

"Well, I've got used to him around after all these years, and he keeps Adrian happy with their school boy jokes and Nat Gubbins. Then he brought this Nancy thing to work in his office ..."

"Thing?" Vitold looked puzzled. "Is there such a strange name?"

"No, you silly," Louise grinned, looking across with her old affection. "She's got a double-barrelled name which Adrian can never remember, so he calls her Nancy Thing."

"Meaning, of course," Vitold gave an answering smile, "that your husband doesn't like her?"

"Meaning just that."

"Stop gossiping you two," interrupted Jeudwine, "or you will miss the big moment."

43

Lights dimmed, there was a flash of scarlet coat as the Toast Master stood to attention.

"Ladies and gentlemen. Pray silence for Mr Bertioni's birthday cake!"

At once the arc lights flooded the entrance, and Harry, the pianist from the Restaurant band, thumped the chords of: "Happy Birthday to you".

"Oh, I hope they won't sing," said Louise, anxiously clasping her hands. "He would hate it."

But Harry continued to play quietly in the background while into the spotlight strode the rotund figure of the old chef Monsieur Le Brun, holding a silver candelabra with lighted scarlet candles. Behind him, four accolites, in the same snowy white linen, pushed a long table on which stood an iced replica of the Hotel Regina.

"I hope it's correct," whispered Moxon to Miss Ballater. "Bertioni will count every window."

"Of course it will be correct," she smiled, touching his hand, "with Mosieur Le Brun in charge."

Moxon smiled back, the touch of Miss Ballater's hand suggested an intimacy, the old days, the old school.

"He's just as good looking as he ever was," she said, turning to watch Bertioni, who had come down from the top table and was standing gazing in admiration at the cake, now isolated in a pool of light in the centre of the room.

"Magnificent," said Bertioni, putting an affectionate arm round the old chef's shoulders. "Absolutely magnificent." Then he bent forward with outstretched finger, pointing to the windows.

"Look, he *is* counting the windows!" Moxon was delighted. "I knew he would."

"Oh, I do hope we can have a look at it before they cut it up," said Mrs Lobb anxiously.

"Cut it up?" Pierre spoke with pontific knowledge. "They wouldn't cut that up. The whole cover is made of hard icing and lifts off and can be kept for years. The cake is underneath and that is already cut into slices so that we all have a piece.

44

And champagne," he added, as waiters removed used glasses, replacing them with champagne glasses, and on the floor by each table putting a silver bucket of ice with its gold-topped bottle.

Pierre, finding the champagne bucket by his side, bent to look.

"Ah, Louise Röederer. Very nice. Don't give us too long a speech now, Norman, I'm looking forward to this."

Mr Jeudwine had joined Bertioni and posed obediently for photographs.

"Just one more, taken from behind the cake, please." Tom Raffin was a little too self-assured for Jeudwine.

"No more." He held up his hand.

"Look," said Bertioni, taking his arm, "There is 215 and 6. That is the President's suite."

Bulbs flashed. "That is the best shot of the day," said Raffin with satisfaction, and led the photographers away.

Louise slipped her hand beneath the folds of the table cloth.

"Now I am happy," she said, touching Vitold's hand lightly, "I hope Jeudwine doesn't come back too soon."

"He is being photographed with your father beside the cake. You did very well, after all, in spite of me holding you back. Jumped that fence and landed safely!"

"Yes, he's agreed to discuss the Front Hall with father now. He was adamant before. You did help though," she added, "I was getting over-excited as usual. You know me so well." She smiled at him, head on one side, seeing more grey in the thick hair than before, the broad forehead a littled lined, eyebrows still dark above those appealing eyes, dark with little gold flecks which seemed always to be changing, like light on water, gentle, sad, amused. A hard Slavic face, tender mouth, how much did she know of him, even now?

"Well?" he queried, eyes quizzical.

"A little greyer, perhaps, but very attractive."

"Am I growing old?"

45

"Oh, no, not you!" Louise sang in her light musical voice, remembering the song she had loved best in "Gigi". At her insistence, Vitold had gone to see it with her on one of his visits, slipping into the darkened cinema, feeling anonymous, holding hands.

Vitold looked at her, remembering.

"All our times together have been happy ones, but this time is very short. Tomorrow I leave for Paris."

"But I haven't seen you . . ."

"Properly?" A shared intimacy, the scene they played together knowing every nuance, Vitold was tender now, no teasing to confuse her.

"We shall see each other, I am hoping. Tonight I am opposite the President's suite on the second floor in 234 and 5. I shall leave the sitting-room door just open, not enough for anyone to notice, but just resting against the lock so that you can push it and slip inside and I shall be waiting for you—as I always will," he added softly, so softly that Louise bent her head to catch his voice.

"Great," said Mr Jeudwine, settling into his chair, held out for him by an attendant waiter, and making a business of getting everything to his liking, touching his glass—which was immediately refilled—tossing aside his napkin, thumping the table and declaring to Bertioni in a loud voice "Great". He turned across Louise to Vitold: "You know, Jan, we could learn a lot from that cake. Have we ever done anything like that in our convention suites?"

"No, sir, but we could," said Vitold, leaning forward to reply and catching a breath of Louise's well-known and well-loved fragrance. Once he had recognised it emanating from a large Daughter of the Revolution at a hotel congress. He had been dismayed and it had fretted him. "This scent," said his heart, "is for fair princesses only."

The moment had come at last. Lobb felt curiously disembodied as if he was floating, cocooned in confidence he felt no qualms at all.

46

"Ladies and Gentlemen," called the Toast Master, "Pray silence for Mr Norman Lobb, Manager of the Works Department for over thirty years and now retired."

As the silence fell, Lobb stood up, caught his wife's anxious gaze and winked.

FIVE

"Once upon a time," Lobb began, "there was an old-fashioned hotel in the heart of London. It was an old-fashioned hotel because it still believed in old-fashioned ideals, and because it had an old-fashioned Manager. He was *very* old-fashioned. He believed in service. He believed in good manners. He believed in excellence at all times. He believed in giving the best to his hotel guests always and at all times, no matter what was going on behind the scenes . . . He really believed the customer was always right.

"Then, just as this old-fashioned hotel began to be known all over the world for these qualities of service given for pleasure rather than for money, there came the second world war. And this was a very good excuse for lazy, undedicated people to drop their standards and take the easy way out with that classic phrase, 'Sorry, there's a war on'.

"But the old-fashioned Manager would not tolerate this attitude for an instant, for he felt very strongly that if the Forces of the Crown could give their lives, be maimed and hurt to protect the lives and property of those left behind, then those very people should respond with the same dedication to keep the flags of kindness, and service, and will to succeed, flying too.

"And so the Manager fought for his old-fasioned ideals and imbued those who were privileged to work under him with such a sense of service that even when the hotel was bombed by the enemy and broken glass lay over the Grill Room tables, eager volunteers swept away the glass, relaid the tables, blocked up the gaping windows with sheets of cardboard; and at 8 am in the morning, breakfast was served as usual.

"And there was a sense of purpose about those years which people still look back upon with a curious nostalgia.

"Then the war ended, and that was when the Manager had his most difficult task of all. For the old-fashioned hotel had suffered considerable damage. The brick walls facing the square had been chipped and were cracked, new window frames were needed and the paint work was in a very bad state indeed. But that was not all, by any means, for the hotel which had so prided itself on the excellence of its fittings, now found it could no longer replace worn items. In the linen room they were down to their last few hundred sheets, for the bed linen was always specially woven in Ireland and that country had not been our ally during the war.

"The famous gold carpet which lined the corridors was now threadbare in many places and there was none left to replace it. Every broken glass or piece of china was a disaster. Apart from all the forms to be filled in to apply for new linen, carpets, glass and china, the Manager knew that the cost of all this would be astronomical.

"But worse than all these worries to the Manager was the lack of spirit in the people. They had won the war against unimaginable and impossible odds. Bravery and dedication had been such that their endeavours would go down in history until the end of time. But something was wrong. Victory had brought with it a shortage of food, more queues, form filling, frustration, and, worse still, no motive.

"However, just when things at the old-fashioned hotel were at their lowest ebb, a fairy godfather appeared in the person of the President of a famous chain of hotels in the United States. He had stayed at the hotel in the past, and though his hotels were modern edifices of the twentieth century, with every new gadget to promote efficiency, he had a fondness for this old hotel and he proceeded to buy it to add to his empire. Being a wise fairy godfather, he did not try to change the hotel too much. He provided treasure from his coffers to refurbish and mend and bring the hotel back to its former glory, and soon visitors from all over the world were flocking there, first of all to see the battle scars, but they soon tired of this and wanted their former comfort; and bit by bit the Manager, who had now become Managing Director, saw that they were not disappointed. And although of the old school, he was an enlightened hotel servant, for he knew that to work well one had to enjoy one's work. So, he started a hotel training scheme for young people and took on as many trainees as he could to teach them in the way of the Regina. And, because he was young in heart and welcomed new ideas in spite of his vast experience, he had a monthly staff meeting where ideas could be freely given and discussed and . . ." Here Lobb paused with a smile, "the Regina's coffee and gateau could be tasted and commented upon. In this way, the young recruits became involved and, like a good team, cared that the standards of the Regina should be protected and maintained.

"And so," said Lobb, looking across at Garbin, the Banqueting Manager, "like all good stories there is a happy ending."

He paused as, at Garbin's signal, waiters swiftly and silently opened champagne bottles and filled the glasses.

"For the hotel prospered under the guidance of the Managing Director, and there came the day when he celebrated his 75th birthday, and there was a great feast and much rejoicing, and all his friends gathered round him."

Lobb bent and picked up his glass.

"Ladies and Gentlemen of this old-fashioned hotel," he said, "please rise and salute your old-fashioned Managing Director. Happy birthday, Mr Bertioni."

There was a moment's silence, then a great rush of sound as chairs were pushed back, glasses raised and the room echoed to:

"Happy birthday, Mr Bertioni!"

Afterwards Bertioni led the clapping, rising to his feet and smiling down at Lobb.

"Absolutely splendid, old friend," said Moxon, leaning across the table to shake Lobb by the hand. "Absolutely right."

Miss Ballater smiled and nodded, "Yes, absolutely right," she echoed. She had been moved.

Lobb drained his glass.

"Told you I was going to tell a fairy story," he said to his wife, "but you wouldn't believe me."

He signalled for more champagne.

"Tell you where you were clever," said Pierre, "and that was not having the champagne poured out first. Get's flat as a pancake by the time the speech is finished—more like bath water."

Robin Wearne, sitting at the end of the top table felt the warmth in the rise and fall of voices below him. For the first time he began to sense the depth of the affection for his grandfather and for the Hotel Regina—certainly among the old staff, and now it was permeating through and there was pride in the new recruits and an eagerness to learn. Even a new recruit, like me, he thought wryly, junior clerk in the Bill Office.

"Sorry you're at the end of the row, Robin," said Andrew Merrin on his right. "Couldn't be helped."

"And I *am* at the bottom of the rung," Robin smiled. He had thick fair lashes. Like his father, felt Merrin, amiable, rather weak, nothing of Louise. Still, he was working well as a manager trainee.

"How are you getting on?" he asked.

"I'm rather enjoying it now, though it always strikes me as rather archaic writing out all those bills by hand with so many computers around. Quite intriguing to see how much people spend on booze," he laughed.

"Anything is better than the Army," he had confided to Charlotte one morning, when they had met in the Front Hall.

"Hardly complimentary to the Regina," she had laughed.

51

"But I was wrong to laugh," she'd told Andrew later. "He is so raw about Northern Ireland. 'It is not a war,' he said, 'it is a mutilation.' He can't get over the pretty girl who lost a hand picking up a grenade put in her garden by the IRA— blood and flesh and pieces of bone blown into the crocheted frill of her blouse where her wrist had been."

Charlotte had been distressed. Robin was her godson and they had always been fond of each other.

"I think writing his book about it got a lot out of his system," she had said, "even if it wasn't such a great success."

"The worst part," Robin was saying, "is when people query a bill asking why there is eleven pounds thirty on it for breakfast when they only had toast, and you spend hours checking with the waiter and invariably find they had late night drinks and it's all been put in with the breakfast." He laughed, "But I'm getting the hang of it."

"I was glad when you joined the hotel," said Merrin, "My two don't seem the least bit interested. Nick wants to be a cricketer!"

"It was Patsy's doing really," smiled Robin, "nothing to do with parents or grandparents. The more they hinted, cajoled, or downright ordered, the less I wanted to."

Downright ordered. Yes that was about it from his father. Even now Robin winced at the scene after he had resigned from the Army.

"Never happened in our family before—always been Army and never gave up." Adrian had poured himself a large whisky without offering one to his son. "Best thing you can do is to get a job right away then it won't look so bad, as if . . ."

"As if I'm a coward?" Robin had asked, white faced.

"No Wearne has ever been called that, so far, that's why you can't hang about, must look as if there is a reason, like joining the family business. Yes, that's it—you can join the Regina. Have to start at the bottom, of course, but it will save face."

"You should have said, 'I thought this was going to be a

friendly argument, old man.'" Louise, trying the light approach quoting Nat Gubbins, their usual panacea, had been waiting for him in the hall, but her eyes had been anxious.

"I think you should have a few weeks holiday first," she'd said.

"Well, I'm not going to join the family firm, that's certain." Robin had been mulish, "I'm going to write a book."

Robin had installed himself in the garden shed at the bottom of the garden.

"Darling," Louise was pleased and practical now that he had started, "let's move out all these deck chairs and things and have it painted for you."

But Robin had preferred the clutter of past summers, and the spider who watched him from a corner above the window, making quick forays out from his cobwebby cacoon, then hanging motionless for hours. As he had stayed motionless too, gazing at the typewriter Louise had lent him, stroking the keys, fiddling with the blank sheet of paper, then transferring his eyes downwards to count the lines in the dusty floor. It was early autumn and it rained a great deal. Soft swathes of misty rain that crept through the garden, hiding the trees and bushes. Drops hung from the ivy outside his window and beyond it the grass was very green. Like Ireland, the wetness and the green. Soon he had slipped back into the past and it was all round him and his fingers hurried to catch it, banging the typewriter keys, feeling the sound like the rev of an engine, pushing him forwards.

"Sorry to disturb you," he'd said cheerfully to the spider who hung above him.

He finished it in the spring and Tom Raffin had been encouraging, had it typed in the office and provided him with the name of a publisher and a large brown envelope in which to post his manuscript. Louise had made it an occasion, opening champagne and insisting on driving him to the post office herself.

The manuscript had been returned rather quickly, in the

same envelope, with a sticky label placed over his carefully typed address.

Robin wore his depression like a uniform. He put it on every morning and took it back to his room at night. Tom, sympathetic, had suggested other publishers, his father made no comment. He had bought a horse, at livery at the local stables, and had suddenly become very jolly. Only Louise lightened the days in bright sleeveless shifts six inches above her knees. She looked very young.

"Darling," she'd telephoned him from the Regina one morning, "I really need your help, desperately, in fact. Mr Jeudwine's niece has arrived and we've been instructed to look after her. She's doing a piece on the 'Swinging Sixties' or 'Swinging London' or something and I have to give her lunch. Do come up and help me, darling. You can have my car."

Robin had a sudden vivid recollection of the serious American girl drinking tomato juice in the bar while his mother sipped a champagne cocktail. Long dark hair scraped back into a velvet bow, round rimless spectacles, neat grey suit—clean and shining as a polished apple, and very confident. They had lunched in the Grill, omelette and iced water, Patsy's choice, and Robin had promptly ordered steak and kidney pudding and a bottle of Beaujolais. He had been polite, charming but unimpressed, until Patsy had informed him that she worked for an American publishing company, then he had swamped her with details of his book.

"Strictly off the cuff, you know, may have to use another name. Officers are not supposed to write about the Army."

Patsy had nodded. "I should like to read it," she'd said solemly. "Maybe we can find a slot for it."

He had taken her out to dinner at the Savoy, and in the American Bar beforehand he remembered how he had leaned forward and removed her glasses.

"Now go down to the Girls' Room and undo your hair—I want to see it loose."

54

Surprisingly, she had got up without a word and he met her in the Front Hall walking towards him shyly.

"You look like a young Judy Garland," he had said, pleased, "I've always loved her."

They saw each other every day during Patsy's month at the Regina. Weekends at home in Hertfordshire with long hours spent in the potting shed correcting his manuscript, with Patsy very sure. The shed had been cleaned and painted on Louise's orders. His spider had gone.

The call from New York had come early one Sunday morning. A matter of fact Patsy. She had someone interested in his book but it was essential for him to come over; and Louise, who had come to listen and was sitting bare-footed on the bottom stair, hugged him and said she'd pay his fare.

As he left two days later, she had handed him a small box.

"Darling, if you get engaged to Patsy, I think you should have a family ring instead of rushing off at huge expense to Tiffany's."

. . . "When you got married?" repeated Merrin at Robin's side.

Robin looked bemused.

"You said Patsy made you join the hotel world."

"Oh, yes, sorry—I was miles away. No, to that question. It was when she got my book published in the States. Said it would look better on the fly leaf if I did something and I was off to hotel school in Switzerland before I knew what had hit me! It was after that we got married." Robin laughed. "One of those large houses on Long Island, with Patsy in white lace and all the trimmings."

"I remember seeing the photographs," answered Andrew, when a cough at his shoulder diverted him.

"Will you be ready, Sir?" asked Mr Garbin.

"Time for the presentation," said Andrew, touching the Chairman's arm, and Adrian turned gratefully. He never felt completely at ease with Charlotte and, having praised Lobb's speech and discussed the menu, conversation had faltered.

In a niche in the wall, usually used for ornate flower arrangements, stood the clock, hidden by blue velvet curtains.

"Mr President, ladies and gentlemen," said Adrian, standing beside it, "I am not going to make a speech—Mr Lobb has stolen all my thunder." There was laughter.

Lobb looked down at his plate, at the rim of marzipan from the cake he had saved for his wife and felt pleased with himself.

"All I am going to do," continued Adrian, "is to pull this cord and the curtains will draw back—and God help the Works Department if they don't," he added affably, amid more laughter.

"No problem in my day," said Lobb to the table at large.

"The curtains will draw back," repeated Adrian, "and reveal the birthday present to which all you loyal friends and colleagues have contribued."

Adrian paused as the curtains parted.

"For Mr Bertioni on his 75th birthday, with our great affection."

"What is it?" asked Mrs Lobb, "I can't see from here."

"Antique chiming clock by Mackie," Lobb, who had grown in stature since his speech, now took Pierre's place as spokesman, "Very fine piece indeed."

Bertioni, amid applause as the curtains parted, had joined Adrian and was examining the clock with reverence. He admired the clock face, the shining brass feet, the curve of the polished wood, then he turned it gently and opened the back, the brass cover delicately scrolled. He touched the pendulum lovingly.

"We can start it if you like," said Adrian, pleased by the delight on Bertioni's face. "We didn't do it before because the chimes would have given it away."

"What time it is?" asked Bertioni.

"Five to ten. It's stopped at a quarter to, so I can just move it on."

Adrian opened the clock face and gently moved the hand.

"Now all we have to do is just swing the pendulum."

"Can I?" asked Bertioni.

He's like a child, thought Adrian. How inspired of Tom to find this. He nodded his head to the Toast Master who banged his gavel.

"Pray silence for your Managing Director."

Bertioni turned, almost it seemed with reluctance, and faced his audience.

"My friends," he said, "This is one of the happiest evenings of my life. I am here in this ..." he paused, smiling, "old-fashioned hotel, which I love so dearly, surrounded by old friends whose service and loyalty have made the Regina what it is. And new ones have come to learn here, become embroiled in our quest for standards, and stayed. Old friends and new, I thank you for this magnificent present. It will be treasured and cherished for always."

Bertioni's voice held a slight tremor and he put his hand in his pocket to feel the silver talisman that never failed him.

"This beautiful old clock," he continued, "which already gives me so much pleasure I do not wish to take my eyes from it, will very shortly chime the hour. I shall hear it for the first time, and when I raise my hand I want you all to listen very carefully, for I want you to hear it for the first time with me."

The silence was so intense that Miss Ballater found herself holding her breath. She saw Bertioni raise his elegant hand and at once there was a small musical chime, followed by another and another until ten had struck.

"With every chime," said Bertioni "I send you a thousand salutes. I shall remember this moment for the rest of my life. Thank you with all my heart."

"Well, that's a success anyway," pronounced Lobb, settling himself comfortably, "Now we can enjoy ourselves."

Pierre put down his glass.

"What's he fussing about now?" he grumbled, catching sight of Garbin hurrying towards the top table. "Always flapping his hands about that fellow."

"Could you spare a moment in the Front Hall?" whispered Garbin in Andrew's ear, "Lord Bearstow is complaining."

How tired he looks, thought Charlotte, watching her husband leave; works too hard and worries too much, but he'll never give up. And what would we talk about if he did?

Merrin found Lord Bearstow pacing the Front Hall still wearing his overcoat.

"Good evening, my Lord. Allow me to take your overcoat. Nothing you need in the pockets?" Andrew signalled for a page.

"Take Lord Bearstow's coat up to his suite and hang it in the cupboard."

Slightly mollified, Lord Bearstow turned to Merrin.

"I have just been refused dinner in your Grill Room," he said.

He was a small man with mild manners but this evening his voice was loud with indignation.

"But this is absurd," replied Merrin, "Who told you this?" He led the way to the Grill Room entrance.

"That little jumped-up Belgian who is on duty at weekends. I always have dinner every Sunday night, bit later than usual today because there was fog on the line. He did say I could have something cold, but that was all. 'Cold,' I said, 'that's not dinner, that's supper—Sunday supper at school after church, brawn and pink blancmange.'" He shuddered at the memory.

"I quite agree with you," smiled Merrin, "we had the same."

"I was looking forward to kidneys," continued Lord Bearstow, almost wistfully. "No heat in the train either."

"You could do with a large whisky and soda," said Merrin, leading the way to a corner table and signalling the wine waiter.

"Will you excuse me for a moment?" he asked, turning away.

Merrin found Pieter, the deputy Grill Room Manager, sitting at a table behind a pillar, smoking a cigarette.

"Well," he asked coldly, "since when has the Hotel Regina refused to serve dinner on a Sunday evening? And don't try and put that cigarette out behind your back, you'll burn a hole in the tablecloth and you've done enough harm for one evening."

Pieter, who was small and vivacious and popular with female clients, found a plate nervously and stubbed out his cigarette. He should not have been smoking and he should not have spent a great part of the evening in the staff bar.

"Everyone else is celebrating, give all the boys a drink," he said, liking to be popular. Down in the kitchens he turned a blind eye to irregularities, and smilingly told a wine waiter and a chef de rang that they could leave early because there was fog. The assistant chef, a sad-eyed Hungarian, was in his office wrestling with a sheaf of figures. The brakes had been taken off and Pieter knew it. He stood, looking sullen.

"You will now go to Lord Bearstow and apologise—using some of the charm you usually reserve for your female favourites, and take his order. I suggest smoked salmon, grilled kidneys and bacon, a very good claret, followed by Stilton. And it is to be served at once."

"But the kidneys will have to be grilled specially," argued Pieter. "We are short staffed in the kitchen. Some of the staff had to go early because of the fog . . . " He was interrupted by a furious Merrin.

"Of course they will have to be grilled specially," he snapped. "Do you think this is a railway buffet?"

Stripped of his calculated charm, Pieter was, thought Merrin, just an incompetent waiter.

"You'd better start putting things together," he warned and, looking back over his shoulder as he walked away, "I shall return to see you have done so."

Walking across the Front Hall, Merrin saw the young receptionist eyeing him anxiously.

"Thank you for sending for me," he said, crossing over to the Reception desk; "that was the right thing to do. All well now, I hope." He smiled, and Crispin, standing erect, felt taller.

What to do about Pieter? Clearly the man was not only

slack and indifferent but could not manage his staff. In the old days he would have been fired overnight. Now all they could do was send him a warning letter, followed by two more if he transgressed again, and then a verbal warning. Then, and only then could he be removed, and in that time how many important clients would be lost? Merrin felt depressed. But at least I didn't escalate it, he thought. I refrained from bursting into the kitchen and letting fly. I don't suppose anyone has been refused a meal in the Regina before, and yet if I had said what I wanted to we would probably have had a strike on our hands.

The happy rise and fall of voices at play met him as he returned to the Banqueting Room. Harry was sitting at the white painted piano playing a selection from 'Bless the Bride'.

Merrin saw Raymond, the Grill Room Manager, across the room talking to Bertioni with energetic gestures and decided not to speak to him. No good could come of it now, it would spoil things. It was everybody's lovely day. He decided to look for Charlotte.

SIX

The Gainsborough Room was a softly lit beehive, the buzz of voices rising and falling with a rhythmic sound. Fresh pyramids of fruit and *friandises* appeared. There was the clatter of coffee cups, the wafting of cigar smoke, the touch of glasses as toasts were made, and now and then the subdued popping of a champagne cork.

"Too much noise with the champagne corks," grumbled Pierre; "should be able to open a bottle without a sound. Sir John was very particular about it. I remember . . ." and he drifted off into nostalgia. No one appeared to listen, but Pierre droned on happily to himself, a light in his eye and a gentle smile straightening the creases round his peevish mouth.

"Let's go and look at the cake," said Miss Ballater, and Moxon smiled and pulled back her chair.

"I must go to the Cloakroom" whispered Mrs Lobb and her husband nodded and wandered off to the little group admiring the clock.

"Ah, Lobb, come and look," called Bertioni, "It's just going to strike eleven. It's an 'old-fashioned' clock," he added, laughing, putting an affectionate hand on Lobb's shoulder.

"I liked your speech very much."

There was a distant whirl of something very old gathering strength, and then the clear chimes as the notes rang out. There was applause from the little group gathered there and Louise, who had been standing quietly among them with her big eyes full of tenderness, threw her arms round his neck.

61

"Now you are happy, darling—it's worked twice!"

She turned to Lobb.

"What a truly wonderful present you all gave him," she said, "but I'm not sure you've done the right thing after all. Instead of standing at the top of the stairs to see that all is well, he'll be rushing back to his sitting room every hour!"

"Mr Bertioni would never do that," said Lobb ponderously, taking her seriously, "never in a thousand years."

Louise looked impishly at Bertioni. "I was only teasing," she said, and they exchanged smiles of love and understanding.

"Your mother," he said quietly, "is getting a little . . ." he paused, bending his head and Lobb moved away with his heavy tread, priding himself on his tact.

"Fretful?" questioned Louise.

"Yes, exactly that."

And you want to move around greeting old staff, sitting where you will, sharing their wine and their friendship without a care in the world. And you shall. "Leave it to me." Louise pressed his hand, turning away with a swirl of the blue dress. Like a kingfisher, and how young she is, thought Bertioni, looking round for Lobb, who had moved out of earshot and was waiting for just such a reunion. He liked to be seen standing with the Managing Director. That was style.

Louise found Robin talking to Charlotte at the top table, which was now nearly empty.

"Darling, please be an angel and go and talk to your grandmother," she smiled at Robin, "Charlotte and I want to have some girls' talk."

"You never draw breath," answered Robin amiably, getting to his feet and moving up the table.

"Mother's become such a bore," said Louise, "She's always so plaintive. If I get like that I hope someone will shoot me."

"I can't see that ever happening," smiled Charlotte. She had a sudden vision of Louise bursting into the Press Office all those years ago, like a shaft of sunshine, pleading to be allowed to work there. And who could refuse her? Certainly not her boss, Graham Venning. She had been quite irresistible then and still was.

"You look so lovely in that dress," she said, "sort of special, as if something very special has happened or—," Charlotte put her head on one side eyeing Louise thoughtfully, "—or is going to happen."

"Father's birthday, of course," answered Louise, turning away to hide her confusion. "And you're looking marvellous. I like you hair done up on top."

"Does it make my face look thinner?" asked Charlotte anxiously.

"It makes you look Edwardian with those ruffles. I should keep it like that."

"You didn't answer the question," sighed Charlotte. "I did try to slim but it never works."

"What about the skipping rope I suggested?"

"Oh, I tried that—complete disaster! I couldn't very well go out in the garden and skip in front of every one so I thought I'd try upstairs and of course the beastly thing got caught up in the chandelier and all the little glass dew drops came off. The Works Department were there all day putting it together again. Andrew was furious," she added mournfully.

Louise's delighted peal of laughter was infectious and Charlotte found herself laughing too. How happy Louise is, she thought.

"What about a dog?" suggested Louise. "You'd have to take him out for walks, though I suppose, knowing you, you'd just ring for a page." She laughed again. "Never mind, you look sweet and Andrew loves you, so I don't really think you can ask for more."

"Have you seen him?" asked Charlotte. "I last saw him going out with a worried expression."

"Well here he is coming back again with a worried expression," answered Louise, who had been watching the scene below her. Now she saw Vitold make his way to greet her father. Bertioni looked pleased and they sat down together at an empty table.

"Do you mind if I go and catch Andrew ...?" Charlotte was already on her feet holding the folds of her velvet skirt in one hand, struggling to move back her chair.

An observant waiter helped her and she flashed him a grateful smile.

"Perhaps I'll ask him for a dog for Christmas," she called to Louise as she hurried away.

I wish she'd put her shoulders back, but she's always scuttled like that, thought Louise, too self-effacing by far, trying to get from one point to another as quickly as possible without anyone noticing her.

"What does she mean—'a dog for Christmas'?" enquired Adrian, who had slipped into the chair beside Louise. "Don't want any dogs here, thank you."

"Only a joke," said Louise. She was resting her chin on her hand and gazing dreamily ahead of her. How thick Vitold's hair grew over his ears, and that dear curve of the back of his head. I would like to have been a sculptor, she thought, turning absently to Adrian.

"I wanted to go back to the country tonight," he was saying, "so that I can go hunting tomorrow. Dodie has a new hunter—might buy him if he's any good. Didn't expect this to go on so long. Let's have a brandy. Waiter!"

"Not for me, thank you," said Louise, "What will you do then?" her voice trembled a little.

"Do you good," said Adrian, giving her a quick look. "You're in one of your nervy moods, old girl, calm you down. Two Armagnac," he said to the attendant waiter. "Everyone has been saying how young you look—and so you do." He patted her hand cheerfully, "And do you know what I have replied? Show's what a good husband I've been!" He looked pink and pleased with himself.

"And so you have," Louise smiled absently. And so he had, leaving her alone, he hadn't clutched, and she had been able to stay Louise Bertioni, her own person.

"And so you have, Adrian,"

She raised her glass and repeated her question.

"What will you do about going home?"

"That's what I am wondering" replied Adrian. "I hope we won't be too late. Do you think you can persuade the parent not to prolong it?"

"I wouldn't even try—it is his big night, after all, and he's enjoying it so much."

Louise left her brandy untouched.

"I should go back tonight," she said indifferently; "it's not that late." And I shall be alone and, her hand touched the brandy glass and trembled. I must not think about tonight, and then it will be easy.

She saw Bertioni leave Vitold and walk over to the piano.

"He's going to ask for his tune," she smiled.

"Who?"

"Father. There—'If I loved you'— Harry plays it so well. I must go down and talk to him."

"You haven't finished your drink," Adrian was irritated; he wanted to sip his brandy and smoke his cigar but not on his own.

"I'll send Tom up,"

Louise found him by the door.

"Oh hulloa," he said. "Nancy has just suggested we have photographs taken of all the tables so that everyone can have a souvenir."

Louise looked at the girl beside him. Tall, very slim with an almost contemptuous elegance, her short hair shiny as a conker. Nose is too big, thought Louise.

"Good idea," she said coolly, "as long as you give everyone their copy and don't make them pay."

"Oh, of course, you were in the Press Office years ago, weren't you?" Nancy Smith-Bretherton had a high voice and spoke rather slowly. "During the war—before I was born," she added.

"Or even a nasty gleam in someone's eye," Louise flashed. "Adrian would like you to join him, Tom—right away."

65

"You'll have to get up very early to beat Louise," Tom laughed at Nancy's sullen face.

"I suppose you're in love with her?"

The calm Nancy found she had an edge to her voice and immediately tried to correct it with a dazzling smile.

"How stupid can you get," Tom walked away. "I'll leave you to arrange the photographs."

Just when he thought Nancy might make a partner, a wife, she did something boringly insensitive.

"I don't know what it is," said Tom, settling himself beside Adrian, "but women are so bloody tiresome. They can never leave anything alone. Is this my brandy?"

"Louise toyed with it. She won't be back. Have ordered some more anyway."

"Was it Violet who couldn't eat fish?"

"No, Violet couldn't eat eggs. It was the other one who couldn't eat fish."

"God," said Adrian, laughing, "what wouldn't I give to have Nat Gubbins back again. Sunday mornings have never been the same."

He looked at Tom.

"What's this about women? Not going to marry Nancy Thing, are you?"

"Nancy Smith-Bretherton, as you well know since her father was one of the chaps in the Regiment."

"That doesn't mean you're obliged to take her on, chum. No sense of humour, that's her trouble."

"Oh, she's all right," said Tom, "jolly good PRO and you must admit she's decorative."

"Too young for you," said Adrian, swirling his brandy gently in its large balloon glass. "She's a nest maker, if you ask me, and in no time at all she'd have it full of eggs."

Tom shrugged his shoulders. "Not my scene." He looked down at his glass.

"A", he said, "I went to see Gerry yesterday. It's rather bad, I'm afraid, going to lose his leg after all the efforts . . .

Didn't want to depress you tonight, but I promised we'd go in with a bottle on Tuesday before the action takes place."

Adrian sighed. "How's Elspeth taking it?" Tom had not called him 'A' for a long time—sign of deep affection—or distress.

"This is it." Tom drained the last of his brandy. "It's all too much. She married him during the war, waited for him until he came back with one leg and couldn't perform any more. Now after all these years of good manners strained to breaking point, he's going to lose the other leg and she's got a complete invalid on her hands. No eggs in her nest. Poor Elspeth."

"God, I get so angry." Adrian closed his eyes briefly as if he had a spasm of pain. "All this 'Never had it so good' talk. Of course they've never had it so good, the pampered youth of today. Mummy didn't give them a third ice-cream when they were four"—his voice went high with mimicry, "so now it's quite understandable and permissible for them to bash old ladies on the head and steal their handbags. Not their fault, poor dears, they were deprived when they were four. Bloody hell, they wouldn't be here at all if it wasn't for the likes of Gerry, and God—he *is* deprived."

Adrian brushed his hand across his eyes and found the lashes were wet.

"Sorry, old man."

"Drink your brandy, A—do you good. I'm with you, you know."

"Time to go home," called Charlotte brightly, appearing behind them, "I've been sent to collect you."

Two faraway faces turned blankly, then focussed on her with dislike.

"Sorry, I've interrupted." Confused Charlotte scuttled away, suddenly near to tears. What did I do? She felt hot, unsure and unattractive.

"Is your uncle in the Navy?" she had asked Adrian at their first and only date together, and he had replied sharply:

"He's Army."

Wartime, and the Dorchester, and the electric organ playing "I haven't time to be a millionaire . . ." She hadn't fitted
even then.

"Silly woman," said Tom, rising. "I bet she can't eat
fish."

They smiled, touched each other briefly, then walked
down to the entrance where Bertioni was saying goodbye to
the departing guests. Adrian took his place beside him,
smiling amiably, pink faced, assured.

"Splendid evening," he repeated to the old familiar faces,
shaking hands firmly. "Splendid evening, eh? One we won't
forget in a hurry."

Bertioni was holding Miss Ballater's hand between his.
"My dear," he said with affection, "your lovely violets and
the colour—the Regina's colour did not escape me. I have
been wanting to talk to you all the evening. Would you be
able to spare a few minutes tomorrow?" Aware of Adrian
beside him, Bertioni lowered his voice and bent forward.

"It is just possible we may have a florists department
again, and I would like your advice."

"Was just thinking about you, Moxon," Adrian extended
his hand, "and wishing you were still here. Have to make an
early start tomorrow—I want my car round at eight o'clock
and I was just wondering who to ask. Don't know the
weekend lot, you see."

"You soon will, Sir." Moxon tried to keep the pleasure
from his voice and squared his shoulders. He felt a great
surge of happiness threatening his control.

"You soon will, Sir," he repeated, "Mr Bertioni has asked
me to come back to do the weekend shift for a while and I
have been delighted to accept."

Adrian looked surprised. Bertioni's idea, of course, but not
a bad one. Nice to have Moxon back again, and he was wearing remarkably well.

"Sir John would have been pleased," he said, smiling and
remembering the bond between the two. "When do you

68

start?" Then added, "Not in time to look after my car, alas."

Moxon stood to attention.

"Leave it to me, Sir," he said. "I start next weekend, but better the day, better the deed. Your car will be ready for you tomorrow morning at eight o'clock."

Forgot to ask him to fill it with petrol, thought Adrian, watching the straight retreating back, but with Moxon, of course, one didn't have to ask.

"Ah, Miss Ballater. Enjoyed your evening? Sorry to have kept you waiting, but gossiping to old Moxon, you know. Delighted to think he is coming back to us."

To Vitold, standing by the door, it seemed as if the good-byes would never end. Often, as a guest left, he would pause, turn and hurry back to Mr Bertioni, grasp his hand again and embark on another reminiscence, old face wreathed in young smiles. Mr Bertioni, for his part, appeared delighted at these extensions to his birthday party, as if any conversation that caused it to be prolonged must be one of great enjoyment.

Beside him, the Chairman, Adrian Wearne, glanced frequently at his watch with ill-concealed irritation; and Jeudwine, who had been watching with a certain amusement, lost patience when Pierre, tears in his eyes, clasped both Bertioni's hands in his and broke into a long and voluble speech.

"Guess this is about all I can take," he said, removing his cigar, which Adrian noticed with distaste was wet with saliva and beginning to disintegrate.

"I've seen the British enjoy themselves, which in itself, I gather, is a rare event, and now I'm off."

"We're quite a happy breed," said Adrian stiffly, but Jeudwine had turned, caught Vitold's eye and was striding ahead. Cocky little bugger. Adrian watched the square figure with the over-padded shoulders march through the door, but we couldn't do without him. If Lincoln Hotels hadn't bought the Regina where would we be?

"Ah, Mr Pierre. Enjoyed yourself, I see. Goodnight. Mustn't keep you."

Adrian shook the limp hand and looked back down the line. Next to Bertioni was a catch of blue and he heard Louise's light laugh. She was prolonging it, too. Damn them.

Miss Ballater followed Moxon into the Front Hall and saw him standing by the Head Porter's desk talking to the night porter. In the old familiar surroundings she waited patiently and contentedly. Those pink chrysanthemums weren't up to much, dreary as washing-up mops.

Moxon turned, saw her, and came across, smiling.

"I may be coming back too," Miss Ballater confided.

Suddenly, in the bustling hall, busy with goodbyes half-finished sentences, moving figures calling and laughing to each other, they were alone, holding hands.

"It will be like old times," said Moxon.

Miss Ballater let her hand rest in the rough firm grasp of the old Head Porter.

"I wonder if our pub is still the same?" she asked.

"Let's find out tomorrow." Moxon released her hand and took her arm instead.

"Now I am going to see you home. Where are you staying?"

Crispin, from his citadel behind the counter of the reception desk, watched the milling throng, the old raincoats over carefully pressed dinner jackets, here and there a British Warm, still presentable, placed away with care, the faint tang of mothballs. But it was the shoes that impressed him most. Old leather they might be, but soled and heeled and shining like the sides of a black limousine.

A night porter came through the swing doors.

"Car for Sidcup," he called.

At once there was further jostling, calls of goodbye, and figures made for the door.

No breathalising or mugging tonight, Merrin had seen to that. Taxis and cars for everyone. Crispin was impressed.

"Watch everything, everyone, all the time. You will learn by the little things . . ."

Bertioni, patriarchial, pausing at the Reception desk one morning, to encourage the new receptionist.

70

"On the stairs coming down I notice a small piece of paper. What would you have done?" he queried.

"Picked it up," Crispin replied promptly.

"Quite right. And complain about it afterwards," added Bertioni, handing over the offending scrap of paper for the waste-paper basket.

Crispin watched the grey-haired woman, elegant in her purple dress, touch hands with the old sergeant major type, and wondered. A housekeeper, perhaps? She looked rather above that. Mrs Spiros, the Night Manager's wife, had been a housekeeper. Mousey little thing, but with a look of sullen temper, she had been imperious when she had arrived earlier in the evening.

"Ring Mr Spiros and tell him his wife is here," she had demanded. Her ancient musquash coat had an orange tinge. She smelt strongly of talcum powder.

Crispin saw her now, crossing the hall beside Spiros, a squat earthy Greek, with a lined, ancient face.

"It's quite absurd for you to go on duty now," she complained.

The creases and folds round the old Greek's left eye seemed to twitch.

Was that a wink at me? Look for the little things. Crispin smiled:

"Good evening, Mr Spiros," he said. "Have you enjoyed your evening?"

"Very much. And now I shall enjoy taking over from you. Mr Crispin has already waited nearly an hour for me, my dear," he said to his wife. "And we appreciate it, don't we? Now I will see you to a taxi."

No wonder he prefers to be on night duty. And there is always that bottle in the filing cabinet to help with the night report. Crispin straightened his shoulders, suppressing a yawn. Suddenly the Front Hall was empty, they had all gone and a gentle lethargy settled over the foyer. It was twenty to one. Sunday with all its purposeful excitement had

71

disappeared. It was Monday morning, a new day, a new week.

"Thank you for staying on," said Spiros, returning quietly. He had a soft, cat-footed tread in spite of his heavy body, walking as if he was holding his breath, so careful was he not to break the night silence.

"Time for a brandy?"

Crispin smiled and nodded, opening the drawer and feeling for the bottle and glasses he knew would be there.

SEVEN

"Darling, it isn't your birthday anymore." Louise looked at the gold hands of the clock, now standing at ten to one. It had been placed in the centre of the mantlepiece in Bertioni's sitting room, the reproduction ormula clock that had stood there for years removed temporarily to a corner of the hearth.

"No, but it still feels like it" Bertioni smiled affectionately, "and we're going to have a very special brandy as a night cap."

He handed a large balloon glass to Tom Raffin who sniffed appreciatively.

"Thank you for bringing up my clock so carefully," said Bertioni, "and for choosing something so beautiful."

Tom perched himself on the arm of the sofa. He felt touched. The old man really was sublimely happy. Quite a risk, really, choosing a clock . . .

"Adrian?" Bertioni held up another glass.

"Oh, well," said his son-in-law affably, "I've reached the point of no return now." He sat down beside Tom.

"Always hunt better with a hangover, anyway,"

"And creme de menthe frappé for Louise." Bertioni was pouring green liqueur on to crushed ice.

"Tart's drink," Tom mocked, watching Louise suck gently through the straw.

"Not any more," Louise retorted mildly. "It's a favourite with at least one member of the Royal family."

Have to be up early to get the better of Louise, thought Tom for the second time that evening. Had she made it up or did she know? Not that it mattered, Louise had had the last word. Sipping his brandy, Tom watched her as she went across to her father and slipped her arm through his. She was looking very appealing in that blue dress, her hair a soft cloud, almost demure, as if she had a lover. Perhaps she had. Tom had often wondered. Theirs had been an odd relationship.

"One of the chaps in the Regiment, I suppose?" she'd queried, when Adrian had first introduced them.

"Tom is going to take over the Press Office," said Adrian, moving over to the sideboard to pour drinks. "And I thought he could stay here until he finds somewhere suitable."

"Here" had been the small house on the river at Richmond, shared with Nanny and young Robin. Louise had made no secret of her resentment. She remembered Tom saying he was allergic to cats, and the next morning she had taken Robin to Harrods and bought him a kitten. Adrian had banished it to the nursery just as he had banished his domestic life away from their own everyday safe one—all the shared jokes and fears and uncertainties of prefect days continued in the safety of Adrian's Regina suite—the study, the oyster shell that kept them safe, not to be prized open by an accusing world.

That fluffy-haired, demure look—Louise had been curled in the window seat of the dining room at Richmond. Breakfast and Sunday bumfs and Nat Gubbins, and for once she had not been irritated by their prattle but had got up to fill coffee cups, enquire about fresh toast, even smile at their jokes. Then she had disappeared upstairs to pack for their trip to the States. Odd how some things stayed with you. He remembered that Sunday morning more vividly than the whole American trip. Those Cadillacs, shining like patent leather, that transported them from plane to endless Lincoln Hotels across the States; Jeudwine blue suited, cigared, snapping orders with a Cagney panache; Adrian permanently truculent after an overdose of lethal Martinis and allergic to the iced water on every table. The monotonous blue suits of the Lincoln employees with two white badges in their lapels, one with their name—DON WHITE OF PERSONNEL HOW ARE YOU? and the other bearing the Lincoln slogan THINK PROFIT. They all seemed light years away, but that Sunday morning was yesterday.

Tom sipped his brandy, still looking back, but I learned a lot from that trip, he mused. I learned that public relations isn't a gentleman's job now. No more of the old boy network, the intimate lunch or dinner . . .

"If you could mention the Regina instead of saying that so and so is staying at a London hotel, we'd be most grateful. I think we could use another brandy, don't you?"

Now the Publicity Office was a news room, sending out a weekly newsletter, more professional and less of the old pals act. And I created it. Tom smiled to himself. He hadn't done a bad job.

"What are you smirking into your brandy for?" asked Adrian.

"I was thinking what a good job I'd done," Tom sipped the last of his brandy, "over the years."

"Of course you have. Anyone querying it? Come on, or we'll be here for that damn clock striking two.

Louise followed the two men to the lift.

"Staying here tonight?" asked Adrian.

"Yes, I'm on the second floor," replied Tom, "I must go down and get my key."

"Oh, key . . ." Louise tried to keep her voice steady. "I've still got the clock key. I must go and give it to father."

"Tomorrow will do," said Adrian, as the lift doors opened.

"No, he'll fuss." Louise knew her cheeks burned and bent her head, fiddling with the clasp of her evening bag. She had hidden the key there for this excuse, but Tom . . . Tom was on the same floor as Vitold, and suddenly she couldn't bear it, the fear, the subterfuge. The back of Vitold's head, that dear curve, the sound of his voice—"After all these years . . ." making their love go on for ever. Suddenly it all disappeared in a routine hotel corridor.

"I won't be a minute." Louise turned and ran back to the

door of her father's suite. When she looked back, Tom was entering the lift with Adrian and they were both going upstairs together.

There was an interval before Bertioni answered her knock and Louise knew where he had been standing.

"Darling, I forgot to give you the key."

"Come in," said Bertioni, smiling, "I don't want tonight to end. It has been so happy. Let's listen . . ."

"No, you must listen to two o'clock yourself," laughed Louise, "and I'll see you tomorrow morning. We'll have champagne." She pressed her cheek against his, "I've been so proud of you."

Walking back to the lift, Louise knew he was still watching her. She turned and waved, blowing a kiss, and waited for him to raise a hand in salute before closing the door. Now she ran, down the stairs, one flight, round the corner, shaded corridor, two neat shoes outside a door, round again and down the next curved stairway, running, away from guilt but nearer to it as she steadied herself on the polished banister. On the third floor she paused for breath, half hidden in the shadows of the stairs, and saw the couple, dark girl in a pale satin dress, stop and raise her face, innocent, yet alive with love, a trusting love, thought Louise, watching the bent head and shoulders of the man, all confident, who laughed and said: "Not so passionate, darling—later—these passages have eyes."

Louise heard their laughter disappear. Yes, they have eyes. She trod slowly down the next stairway, hand clasping the rail as if in a hidden prayer to be halted. Here it was, the second floor—room 234. On the wall opposite the head of the stairs she saw the signs—234 and 235, on one side; 215 and 216 on the other. A long way to the end of the corridor, a long way to be seen on the way to and from the lift.

Louise sat down on the last stair and waited in the shadowy solitude of a hotel corridor in the early hours of a Monday morning. Nothing stirred, nothing moved, but it all might come to life at the touch of a lift button—Tom, Mr Jeudwine, a night manager on his rounds.

Louise bent her head. It's not my scene. I've betrayed him. I should be upstairs and we'd be sipping Ovaltine and I'd be curled on the sofa and we'd laugh and go over the whole evening together, bit by bit. It was what he would have loved ... What was it about Ceasar's wife? She must be above suspicion.

Vitold, walking to the lift for the third anxious time, found Louise still huddled on the bottom stair. He saw the startled eyes as she sprang up and held her gently in his arms.

"Poor Louise," he comforted, his eyes concerned. "It is not for my Princess to be lurking in hotel corridors. How bad of me."

He led her quietly down the passage to his open door.

"Tonight we will just talk together—for a few minutes, please. I have so much to say to you."

Once the door had shut behind them, Louise began to recover. She smiled and the light returned to her eyes.

"My courage is beginning to return," she said, putting her arms round Vitold's neck, stroking the back of his neck, nestling against him.

"Napoleon once said that he had rarely met with two o'clock in the morning courage." Vitold stroked her hair and led her gently into the next room.

"That must have been courage in war." Louise kissed him, then broke away to sit on the edge of the bed.

"No, moral courage." Vitold knelt before her, taking both her hands.

"*Quant au courage moral, il avait trouvé fort rare, disait-il, celui de heures après minuit.*"

Louise listened, loving the sound of his voice, but understanding little.

"Such lovely language. I wish I spoke it better." She sighed. "I used to once. We went to Paris, after the war, father and I, just the two of us and we made a pact to speak only French to each other ... Oh, we laughed so much! Father speaks perfectly, like you, and so quick. '*Lentement, lentement,*' I'd keep saying, and he would start again slowly ..."

77

She always comes alive when she talks of Bertioni . . .
Vitold, watching Louise's face, now full of animation, smiled
with her. She was relaxed, so perhaps he could make the
suggestion that had been in his mind all the evening.

"I am going to Paris tomorrow," he said.

"It is tomorrow," sighed Louise, then sadly: "it is tomorrow
now and there is so little time."

"You could come too."

"Me?" Louise, wide-eyed, looked puzzled, "but Vitold,
how could I?" Then happiness overtook her and she laughed,
throwing back her head. "Oh, my love—how wonderful that
would be."

"And shall be." Vitold was serious, holding her hands so
tightly that Louise stopped laughing, sat up and saw the truth
in his dark eyes.

"You mean it, don't you?"

"Of course. Why not? Tonight our splendid President told
me how dull was his suite—pea green, was I think the word
he used. He said that you were now in charge of furnishings—
is that right?"

"Oh, dear." Louise drooped. "Yes, I am, have been for
ages, but it's awfully uphill work trying to make them all
change. We haven't got this far yet—we're on four, the
Works Department insist on doing decorations floor by floor
. . . I do hate being criticised," she said with a mocking shrug
as if at her own foibles.

"He wasn't criticising you—just the Regina, which he
considers old fashioned and," Vitold hesitated, searching for
the right word—"and contained."

"Contained?" Louise puzzled

"You know what I mean—inside, not wanting to get out."

"I think you mean insular," Louise replied solemnly, and
Vitold laughed, bending forward to kiss her.

"Clever one. Insular, of course, and don't sound so stiff
when you say it. I approve of this insular, this staying as you
are and not coming out. How I would like to turn back the
clock to insular in my own land, but the New World, they

78

want change all the time, like these dreadful popple popple crackle packets for breakfast instead of real food."

He stopped at Louise's merriment.

"Darling, I'm sure it isn't popple popple crackle, but popple is a lovely word," she laughed, "and you are a lovely dear man and," she hesitated, looking down at her hands still entwined with his, "and I am so very fond of you."

Tom pressed the button by the lift, saw the light at the second floor and watched it flash upwards, becoming stationary at the seventh. He had not meant to stay so long, but the comaraderie with Adrian had been so pleasant and undemanding that time had slipped away until Adrian, pouring himself a glass of iced water, said, "Well, that's my lot"; adding, as if only suddenly aware she was not there, "What could have happened to Louise?"

"She's with beloved Dad, that's what." Tom stood up. "I've enjoyed this evening. Don't forget about Tuesday."

Yes, it had been a good evening all round, though Nancy wasn't going to be pleased. He'd rather left her in mid air.

Tom waited for the lift doors to open and saw the flash of blue, the tousled hair and smudged lipstick in a quick startled glance.

"You two have been gossiping," said Louise quickly, hurrying past with downcast eyes to hide her confusion.

She fumbled with the key, letting herself in quickly, and heard Adrian's voice from the bedroom.

"Is that you? I've just gone to bed so don't put the light on."

"Don't worry, I'll undress out here," Louise called back, and wondered how she would undo the zip fastener on her dress. Vitold had done it up for her, lifting her hair and kissing the nape of her neck . . .

In the sitting room there was the smell of old ash trays and brandy. Aftermath of an evening. Louise wrinkled her nose in disgust, pulled off her shoes and went out, shutting the door. In the bathroom she gushed water into the bath, emptying the Floris bottle with abandon so that the fragrance of Stephanotis rose with the steam that misted the walls. She grappled with the back fastening of her dress, right arm bent back against her spine, smiling at her contortions.

"How do single girls manage?" she had once said to Vitold, struggling before he came to help her.

"Quite simple. They should not be single."

Then her searching fingers found the top of the zip. She pulled gently and was free, blue chiffon a pool on the tiled floor. She wiped the long mirror, seeing her pale figure damply blurred. Feeling beautiful, too beautiful for the plastic confines of a bath cap, she pinned up her hair and lay back in the warm, scented water, remembering.

"That was properly." How happy she had felt, all the strains had gently fallen away.

"No, properly is to stay with you all night so that I can turn in my sleep and stroke your soft skin and wake and know that tomorrow we will love again. That is properly."

I love the way Vitold says properly, Louise thought, stretching with the sensuousness of a contented cat, each syllable pronounced carefully and slowly. Tomorrow it could be properly if she agreed to go to Paris. She was aware her hair had become loose and floated wetly round her neck, and was too contented to care. Later, she rubbed it lazily with her bath towel, which she trailed behind her, as she felt her way into the darkened bedroom. The cool kindliness of sheets. In a few minutes she was asleep, wet tendrils of hair clinging to the pillow.

In the lift Tom realised he had not collected his key and pressed the button for the ground floor. He would have a look at the house list too. Louise had come from the second floor, not from Bertioni's suite. Very interesting, and intrigued, he walked into the sleepy silence of the Front Hall where he saw the Night Manager beckon to him from the reception desk.

"I am glad to see you," said Mr Spiros. "That singer

Alicia, whatever her name is, she's on her way. They've just rung from Heathrow."

"Alicia Berger? But she's not due until tomorrow."

"No, well, she's come on her own, without her manager and the pianist, and is in a state, so our chap said."

"Is her suite ready?" asked Tom.

"Of course, no problem there, but there won't be any flowers. I was just wondering when you came in whether I could nick some from the birthday party." Spiros grinned, and at once the old face, wrinkled like a walnut, sprang into animation.

Bet he still chases them, remembering Spiros's past reputation, Tom gave him an amused glance. "Come on, then," he said. "Got your pass key? And bring a page."

Inside the empty Gainsborough Room the carpet was swept, chairs neatly stacked, only the top table remained, green baize top, on it a collection of flower arrangements, stacked side by side.

"That florist shop will collect them all tomorrow," said Spiros, "and flog 'em again. Bit of a racket, if you ask me."

"Which suite has she got?" asked Tom.

"Fourth floor, one of the newly decorated ones that Lady Wearne did. All pink."

"Then we'll have the roses," said Tom. "Two lots, I think."

Upstairs, Tom played with the lights until he had a soft ambience. He liked the deep pink velvet curtains, the paler pink and white striped sofa; and the roses, although a little soft, looked well on the mantlepiece and the corner table. He filled a glass from the bathroom and topped them up, mopping up spilled water with his silk handkerchief, then rang for the floor waiter. Tom, agreeably surprised by the prompt knock at the door, order a jug of iced water, a bottle of Perrier and, as an after thought, Bollinger and a plate of smoked salmon sandwiches. Leaving all the lights on, he went downstairs.

"Well done," he said to Spiros, standing as tall as his

square frame could manage, "those flowers made all the difference. Now let's have a look at your house list."

"Anyone in particular?" asked Spiros, handing over the sheet of foolscap.

"I was wondering who was on the second floor," Tom said casually.

"Only the President. Surprised they didn't put him in one of the newly-decorated suites on the fourth or fifth, but Mr Bertioni insisted."

"Method in his madness," Tom answered, running his finger down the list. "If the President finds his suite needs refurbishing, he will have to OK the costs."

"Though this be madness, yet there is method in it," corrected Spiros and Tom looked up and laughed.

"Shakespeare, I suppose?"

"Of course, it nearly always is," said Spiros, breaking off a conversation he would have enjoyed to look towards the revolving doors.

"You ought to go in for one of those quiz things," said Tom, resuming his look down the list. Only Jeudwine and Vitold and a few unknown names. "You'd win hands down."

Spiros was standing stiffly as a pointer looking at the doors, still stationary.

What would we do without him, Tom thought, night after night sitting here with his bottle of brandy in the filing cabinet and his *Oxford Dictionary of Quotations*, happy as a lark and never missing a thing.

"And there arrived a new admired guest," quoted Spiros, as the doors spun round.

"I only know 'better to travel than arrive'," answered Tom.

"And you may well be right," Spiros raised his bushy grey eyebrows in surprise and walked forward.

Through the doors had emerged a small fair girl in a loose black coat, white chiffon at her neck, long hair floating to her shoulders, with the clean scrubbed look of an American. She

82

was walking carefully in stockinged feet and in her right hand she carried her shoes.

"Good evening, Miss Berger," said Spiros, inclining his head, "I trust the journey was not too arduous?" He pronounced Berger with a soft G, and Miss Berger said with the bored air of one who has repeated the same line many times:

"Hard G, as in ham."

Spiros, leading the way to the Reception desk, looked bewildered, but Tom grinned.

"Allow me to take your shoes, Miss Berger," he said, accenting the name correctly.

"You get it, huh?" she smiled in spite of her weariness. Then to Spiros, "I don't know about arduous, it was just sheer torture, squashed together, and when I took off my shoes to try and sleep I couldn't get them on again."

"We expected you tomorrow," said Spiros mildly, handing her the black and gold pen. "If you would please sign here. But all is ready for you."

"Yes, I know, but I just hopped on a plane on my own—sort of impulse, you know?"

Spiros was sympathetic. "Of course," he said with the air of a kind father, "and this is Mr Raffin, the director in charge of our Public Relations."

"Hi!" said Alicia Berger, liking the look of the tall, dark Englishman. In his fifties, perhaps, and knew what it was all about.

"I hope you're not going to have photographers around," she said, looking down at her feet, "I'm really bushed."

Spiros led the way, Tom followed, still carrying the shoes which he had already noticed had an exclusive Italian label.

"Why, this is just darling," exclaimed Miss Berger as the door opened on the soft lights, pink furnishings and the two large flower arrangements of pink and red roses.

"I think I'll just have a tub and go right to bed." She held out her hand to Spiros, "Thank you so much for your lovely welcome."

Spiros indicated the linen-covered table against the wall.

83

"A little refreshment, Madam, should you so wish."

Old bastard, thought Tom, half expecting the leonine head to turn and see a wink from those deep-set eyes, furrowed in wrinkles.

"Perhaps you would rather have some warm milk?" Tom suggested.

Miss Berger, who was already disturbing the cress surrounding the sandwiches, turned.

"Warm milk with smoked salmon—you must be joking!"

"In that case," replied Tom, "I shall open the champagne."

"This is my favourite food." Alicia Berger waved a sandwich as she padded into the bedroom. "Never tastes so good in the States," she called over her shoulder, "Guess it's your bread."

"My favourite, too," Tom called back. "I've just realised I'm hungry,"

She returned almost immediately, having removed her coat, wearing a pleated black skirt and white silk shirt, a single gold chain round her neck. Her hair still fell untidily and gave her a vulnerable air.

"You don't look tired," said Tom involuntarily, handing her a glass of champagne.

"Well, that's not bad after the day I've had." Miss Berger looked pleased and settled herself on the sofa with her legs on a cushion.

"Are you going to drop grapes into my mouth?" she asked.

"Of course," replied Tom sitting down beside her with the plate of sandwiches. She had a soft skin, opaque, and large eyes the colour of light brown pansies, the kind they used to have in a garden at home. Tom remembered a sunny morning long ago. The grass had just been cut and the sharp fragrance mingled with the flowery scent his mother always used. She was wearing a print dress and a floppy linen hat to shield her fair skin.

"Why do you have those old brown pansies in the garden?" he had asked. "I like the pretty mauve ones."

"Oh, darling, I love the brown pansies so much more. They have more depth, like loving doggy eyes ..."

"Something sad?" A light hand touched him and Tom blinked, then looked up. His mother had died years ago, crumpled and thin, the memory still hurt. Only Adrian had understood.

"I was thinking of my mother. She loved brown pansies and your eyes made me think of them—and of her. I'm sorry."

"Why should you be sorry? That is the nicest thing that has been said to me for a long time." She played with the stem of her glass, sensing the Englishman's inborn fear of showing his feelings, eyes lowered to spare his embarassment.

But Tom, to his surprise, felt comfortable and at ease. Alicia Berger had a funny little bungey nose, rather sweet, like a round india rubber. Tom was smiling as he went to refill the glasses and sat down again on the edge of the sofa.

"What is your name?"

"Tom"

"And I'm Alicia. I expect you are wondering what I was doing arriving a day early with only one suitcase—and," she laughed, "no shoes."

"It had crossed my mind."

"Well, you see, I was all burned up. I'm the one who is opening at your Palladium on Thursday. I'm the one who has to look great, sing great and just be great. But to hear Milton talk—he's my manager—you'd think the whole thing revolved round him. And little Ronny, who's been my pianist since forever and who knows me better than I know myself, why, he suddenly started saying, 'You can't sing that Lissie, Milton says it isn't box office,' and so on and so on ..." Alicia waved both her hands, sprinkling raindrops of champagne on to her skirt, which she appeared not to notice.

"So I just left the apartment in what I stood up in and grabbed a suitcase and my passport and took a taxi to the airport and in no time at all I was on a plane—don't ask me how." Alicia sighed, "I just wanted a little boosting, that's all, it's quite an ordeal, your Palladium you know, and such an honour."

"You'll be terrific."

"Do you always wear a tuxedo and greet guests in the early hours of the morning?" asked Alicia, as if she hadn't heard.

"Only special ones," smiled Tom, and she laughed.

"That's what I knew you would say, and would I have been disappointed if you hadn't! Now I'm going to bed to sleep and sleep and sleep."

She stood up, small beside Tom, and reached up to brush her lips across his cheek.

"Thank you for everything."

Tom had a strange feeling of belonging—not to now. To the past? He was not sure, feeling confused, but happily confused and wondered if he wasn't rather drunk. Surprising if I'm not after an evening like this, he thought. "Mind over matter", as Adrian would say. Tom made a conscious effort to clear his brain, then he said firmly:

"Do they know where you are? You have a photo call on Wednesday morning, you know."

"Oh, gee, yes. Well, I guess they don't know." Alicia worried her hair across her forehead with a small plump hand and sighed. "I just walked out like I told you."

"Let's send a cable." Tom sat down at the desk, the reticent Englishman in command again. "Name? Address?" He paused. "How about: ARRIVED SAFELY HOTEL REGINA LONDON. STOP. AND WHERE ARE YOU?"

Alicia laughed, wrinkling up her nose.

"I love it. Will you send it for me and ask them not to put any calls through until I ring. And Tom, will I see you tomorrow?"

"Of course." Tom closed the door behind him and made his way once more to the Front Hall, more silent than ever, with the air of a deserted station. The Reception desk was empty, but behind the Enquiry Office counter a pale uniformed clerk watched him with an impassive face.

"I would like you to send this cable please," said Tom

86

handing over the piece of paper; "and charge it to Miss Berger."

The clerk, unsmiling, pushed across a cable form.

"Fill this in please. And what number is Miss Berger?"

For a moment Tom was surprised, then he frowned angrily.

"How long have you been at the Regina?"

"I'm a relief." The reply was morose.

"Well," replied Tom, pushing the cable form and his piece of paper back across the polished counter. "Relief or not, you have a great deal to learn. First of all, you always say 'Sir'. Secondly, the guest is always right, and thirdly, the Regina prides itself on the pleasant manner of its staff. Got that?"

"Yes." A pause, then as Tom waited, a reluctant 'Sir' followed.

"So now you will fill in and send this cable as I asked you in the first place and see that no telephone calls are put through to Miss Berger until she says so."

The clerk made an elaborate study of the house list, running his finger down the list, then lifted his head to say triumphantly:

"No Berger here—Sir."

"Of course there isn't, she only arrived an hour ago, which you should know as you were on duty."

Tom knew he was being provoked and lost his temper.

"Take your finger out, man, and give me my key. The name is Raffin, and if you don't know who I am you had better find out."

He strode away, suddenly very tired. He wished he had not lost his temper, one shouldn't with the staff—never knew where it might lead. All the same, the fellow was bloody insubordinate and needed watching. Must find out more about him from the Staff Manager. God, I'm tired. Inside his room Tom undid his tie, looked at his wan face in the mirror and yawned loudly. Good thing we don't demand overtime, he thought—I'll tell Adrian tomorrow. But for the first time since his school days, Tom knew there was something he could not tell Adrian. It was too new, too cobwebby—dew drops on cobwebs, mustn't push them away and break them.

Alicia wasn't beautiful. Sweet little face, though; soft petal skin and those pansy brown eyes. He felt comfortable with her, no, that was not the word—companionable. Tomorrow, in a few hours time, or today, what have you, I'm going to have a hangover and Nancy will be frosty. Tom fell into bed. I'm looking forward to Monday, he thought drowsily, it's beckoning in a rather friendly way.

EIGHT

Spiros returned from the private room next door to the staff dining room, where heads of departments followed Army rules and ate in their own Mess. This morning he had eaten poached egg on haddock, drunk four cups of strong tea and read most of the *Daily Telegraph*.

"Good piece in Peterborough," he said cheerfully at the Enquiry Office desk. "I'll have another copy, please."

"What of?"

"*The Telegraph*, of course," replied Spiros, looking at the clerk with a slight frown. He was not sure about this new chap, didn't fit somehow.

"Haven't you read it?" he asked, rubbing a hand across his chin and feeling the morning beard.

"Only read the *Mirror*," was the response.

"Well, you'd better read about Mr Bertioni's party in the *Telegraph*; and see you have plenty of copies, there's bound to be a run on them."

The clerk turned to look up at the clock behind him.

"I'll leave a note for the day staff," he said, in a voice so lacking in animation that the elderly Greek grew angry.

"It is over ten minutes until you are off duty," he said with a deliberate slowness to calm himself, "So as I am in charge, you will do what I say and order some more copies."

The clerk gave a slight shrug of his shoulders.

"How many?" he asked.

"Use your initiative." Spiros picked up his paper and was about to leave when for the first time he saw a flicker of expression on the pale face, the eyes very round, alarmed, the iris an island surrounded by white. "Poached-egg eyes—bad sign to see the white all round." Old Ted used to say that over his drink in the staff bar. 'Balmy, that's what. If you ever see anyone with the whites of their eyes showing all the way round the pupil, you can bet on it—balmy.'

"Well?" said Spiros, watching.

"In Leisure Lines we weren't allowed to make decisions. Everything had to be done through the central office."

"This is the Hotel Regina, not Leisure Lines, and as you are acting head of the Enquiry Office at this moment you are expected to make your own decisions, not have them made for you."

Leisure Lines! Lots of little box-like rooms, all decorated the same; make your own tea, carry your own luggage, no personal attention, just a number on the computer. Whatever was the fellow doing at the Regina?

"Order thirty," he said shortly, "that should cover you," and he watched the flicker of relief on the palid face. That's right, Spiros grumbled to himself, obey orders to the letter and not a jot more. Eight to five and don't give one halfpenny to the other side. Them and us. What's the point, he thought angrily, how can you enjoy your work if you don't take part in it, give something of yourself? He was annoyed with himself too for being provoked by a nonentity clerk who couldn't even grow a proper moustache without a graze of pimples. And who wouldn't have been put in charge if there had not been an emergency, number two on holiday just when Bob was sent to hospital with a perforated ulcer.

"Too much of that Greek brew of yours in the small hours," Bob had smiled from a white face stiff with pain. "Don't forget to come and see me."

Should be alright to go now, thought Spiros. I'll call in tonight and tell him about the party. When he left his desk he looked back and saw the pale clerk had gone.

'*Tant pis*', he said to himself. And now I must return to another breakfast, fatty bacon and fried eggs so overdone they'd be hard boiled; but the coffee was better since he had bought Ruth the new perculator, and he endured it cheerfully so as not to hurt her feelings, feelings that were always waiting to be hurt, knowing that in a few hours he would be back where he belonged, behind the Reception desk at the Regina. He was heavy bodied, grey hair still dark at the roots, brush stiff, a nocturnal creature who lived by his senses. And now, on this drab November morning, making his way towards the tube station, he was aware of an unease, sniffing, fearing danger.

Standing at the bus stop, mackintosh collar turned up and cap pulled down over his eyes, the clerk watched Spiros walk by. The bus approaching had the wrong number, so he held back, eyes following the disappearing figure. He shivered suddenly—goose flying over your grave, his mother used to say. Not that he saw much of her out working in the factory. No father, killed in an accident, she said, but he had no childhood memories of Dad. Dead loss, most of them were, she said; boozed, left without paying the rent, always looking for an escape and shouting if they stayed. He'd taken refuge in his school books—Old Owl Eyes, they called him, baiting him, but he'd learned to keep clear of the school playground, spending his break on the plastic seat of a lavatory, waiting for the school bell.

The exams had been easy, no problems, best results in the school and a job lined up as a pageboy in the Enquiry Office of a big hotel chain. His mother had come alive then.

"I'm really proud of you, love. Give them down the road something to think of. And you're going to have a proper suit to go in, I don't care what it costs and you don't have to worry about the coupons."

New suit, new job, new surroundings . . . it was quite easy, you just did what you were told. The years slipped away and he grew taller and became a clerk. It was alright until you left work—what did you do then? No one told you what to do with leisure.

There was a pub round the corner where they all used to go and, because it was routine, he would go too and sit and drink his beer on his own, but it was better than going back to the empty flat straight away. Until the evening the big Irish chap with the curly hair—Terry they called him—knocked over his glass with a wave of his arm in a graphic replay of a story heard many times, but received with applause yet again.

"Sorry, boyo. I'll fill it up."

"It doesn't matter," he'd been confused, suddenly in the limelight.

"Knock over someone's drink and not replace it? Men have been shot for less!"

The clerk, who had a morose nature and avoided physical contact with people as much as he could, found he did not shrink from the large sweaty arm flung round his shoulders.

"This is my mate, Liam—God's gift to the building trade!"

The red-haired youth in stained dungarees had laughed. He was younger than the boisterous Terry, with a good-humoured face and a love of companionship. It was always Liam who saw him first, and shouted:

"Here's our friend!"

They sat at a round table with a red plastic top as far away from the bar as possible, because Terry liked the mini-skirted barmaid and it was the only way he could see her legs.

"Same again, me darlin'." he'd call, and Liam would laugh and the clerk would pay and they would ask him about his job. From beer they graduated to Irish whisky and the clerk found himself confiding that he had a fortnight's holiday to come and that he did not know what to do with it.

"We'll take you to Ireland with us, boyo. Just for a week, mind you, but you can do us a favour first, eh Liam?"

Terry had made it all sound very simple. All he had to do was to sign on at the Hotel Regina for a week as a relief Enquiry clerk; no problem, they were short of staff and would be glad of someone with his experience. And while he was there behind the Enquiry Office desk, he could do them a favour, just draw a map of the Front Hall with the exits and the counters and the main entrance so that their film director friend could get his film set right, the Regina being a stuffy lot who had refused permission for photographs.

"A film?" The clerk asked, excited.

"Yes, like Grand Hotel, before your time, of course, but it's going to be a great, and you'll get a ticket for the first night, having helped. Might even get your name on the credits if you do a good job, eh Liam?"

"How will I get the job?"

"Just say you have a week's holiday and want the extra money. No problem with your references."

It had been difficult at first, the counter at the Regina was busy and he was constantly in view of the other clerks or the pageboys, then half way through the week he had been put in charge of the night shift and for periods during the early hours he had been on his own. Now he had done it and it was a good drawing, he was sure it was good. Fingering the folded envelope in his mackintosh pocket, the clerk saw a cruising taxi and hailed it. To hell with waiting for buses, he'd done a favour for his friends and they were all going to Ireland together.

"There'll be a few thick heads this morning." Andrew Merrin, eating eggs and bacon with the night report propped against the coffee pot, looked across at Charlotte. "And how are you?"

Dear thin face, she thought, all lined and drawn with over-work, but when he smiles it seems to come from deep inside and all the lines disappear.

"I rather wish I had a hangover," she answered, smiling, "then we could have champagne before lunch."

"Stop talking about drink before we've even finished breakfast." Andrew sipped his coffee. "Anything in the *Telegraph*?"

"Yes, a nice write-up about the party in the Diary saying Bertioni is the doyen of hoteliers, but no picture unfortunately."

Charlotte sighed, "There's also an unpleasant little paragraph tucked away on page two saying the IRA have announced they are going to step up their activities, with particular regard to London."

"That's something we can do without," Andrew looked up, frowning. "We might end up having to search people's handbags as they come in." He turned the pages of the night report.

"Alicia Berger has arrived—she wasn't expected until this afternoon."

"I expect old Spiros coped." Charlotte poured coffee, spilling some on the spotless cloth.

"Oh, damn! Wouldn't you think I could pour coffee without spilling it after all these years?"

"Take the lid off—I keep telling you. Tom Raffin was the one who coped; he escorted her upstairs and stayed some time. He and Spiros pinched some flowers from the party for her." Andrew laughed. "More coffee, then I must go—and take the lid off."

"I hope he was nice to her."

"Who?"

"Tom—I mean . . ." Charlotte was running away from the top table, cheeks flushed with humiliation. "He can be awfully off-putting," she floundered, "to women. Louise says he is awful to Nancy Thing . . ."

"Oh, Louise. She's just feminine. For years she has resented Tom living with them, and as soon as he looks like getting married and leaving she wants him to stay."

Andrew went across and kissed Charlotte.

"I like you in that pink housecoat," he said, "and last night you looked like a bonny peach."

"Oh, Andrew," Charlotte laughed, loving him, "How can a peach be bonny?"

"I don't know, but you were."

At the door he turned: "By the way, you can order that champagne. I'm going to have a bloody awful morning and I shall need it to celebrate *not* having a strike on my hands or to drown my sorrows because the Grill chef has resigned."

I'm so lucky. Charlotte looked at the thin slivers of butter on their bed of ice, the toast wrapped in the white napkin and there was a choice of marmalade or strawberry jam. I can't resist any of it and Andrew likes me as I am. She pushed aside the grapefruit—it looked sour in its glass bowl, and relaxed, thick butter on toast, jammy fingers on the *Telegraph* and no washing up.

Andrew decided to walk downstairs.

"The only exercise I ever get," he would say, his thin face creased in a self-deprivative smile, but his staff knew better. The hand rail of the banisters, the edge to the carpeted stairs had to be as immaculate as the Front Hall and nothing would miss him.

"You're as bad as Bertioni," Charlotte had laughed at him. "Dust on the back of the lift cage! What a fuss! Who would see that anyway?"

"I might—and did. A valuable client who had been told by his doctor to walk and not take the lift, might. A pretty girl on her way to an assignment might—no, cancel that, she'd have other things on her mind."

"Such as?" Sometimes Charlotte would laugh and tease him, and Andrew would remind himself that he had a loving wife and two teenage sons who knew how to play cricket, so what more could a husband want? The odd, mad magic, the face seen in a crowd—across the room—wasn't there a song he had loved? To meet it and want it, Andrew gave a deep sigh, and to resist it, for that was always what he would have to do.

In the Front Hall he saw Lord Bearstow, bowler hat, umbrella, highly polished shoes—our valet, I hope, he thought.

"Good morning, my Lord," he said, smiling.

"Ah, Mr Merrin, I'm very glad to see you. Afraid I was a bit off last night—public transport and all that, bit frayed round the edges. Wouldn't have bothered you when you had a party on, but I did have a capital meal after you took over. Trouble is, you know," his old eyes were watery and very light blue, "I've come to rely on the Regina—don't think much of things as they are now, but somehow being here has always made me feel my standards were worthwhile and not something to be ashamed of."

Merrin was touched. "I hope we shall never fail you."

"You never will if you keep the discipline. Don't want it now, the young think they know best. Good luck to them, give them a chance, but they will never succeed if they don't recognise discipline. You've got to learn from the old ones, they had to learn before. All right, if they've got something better to offer—let's see it. We've given them the chance with all this permissive society and are they happier? Have you ever seen a vixen with her cubs in a field in the evening sunlight? I have. She watches them, lets them play and have fun—there's nothing so pretty as fox cubs gamboling in a buttercup field," the old man smiled, "but when it's time to go she gives them a backhander, barks at them. Discipline, you see, she knows that a few minutes longer and they might be in danger; she knows, they don't, but they obey because they trust her."

For a moment Merrin was transported to an early summer evening, scents of hay, the chuckle of a cuckoo, egg laid in some unsuspecting nest, winging into the fading sky—a far away echo of childhood, which he repressed quickly.

"Where is your overcoat, my Lord?" he asked.

"Oh, it seemed warm today and I'm only going to the House, and anyway I can't be bothered to go all the way upstairs."

"It is a grey November day, not summer, my Lord."

Merrin beckoned to the Hall porter.

"Go upstairs and fetch Lord Bearstow's overcoat," he commanded, and if he says, what room or where is the key, he thought, by God I'll fire him.

"Certainly, Sir."

Merrin conversed a little, and listened a great deal more, on the topic of the weather and how it was not what it used to be and all the time his eyes watched the purple-uniformed porter walk to the lift and waited for his return. Within five minutes he was back.

"Your overcoat, Sir."

Lord Bearstow, helped into his coat, fastened the top two buttons, and smiled at Merrin.

"Now you see what I mean," he said, fastening the third button, his head bent so that Merrin had difficulty in hearing, but it sounded as if he was saying, "Only the Regina has this service."

And long may it remain. Andrew walked towards his office, his mind now switched to the Grill management of last night. Raymond, the Grill Room Manager, would be at the morning conference, but it would not be politic to mention it in front of the other heads of departments; though by the time the staff bar opened last night's trouble in the Grill kitchens would be common knowledge. Raymond was weak on discipline, no question of it. Charming with the ladies, all admiring smiles, and got his sums right in his little office when he added up the day's takings. He knew how to make a profit, but his staff ran rings round him. What we need is a good number two, with no frills, who must know the union rules from A to Z.

Sitting down at his desk, Andrew sighed. Union rules—I suppose somewhere along the line we brought it on ourselves, but now the unions were like lemmings, leading their members headlong over the cliff.

"Don't sigh yet, Mr Merrin, you haven't even seen the post!"

Andrew looked up at the pleasant face of his secretary, silk shirt, cashmere cardigan, a younger edition of old Miss Hamer, but with humour.

"Don't tell me."

"The Bill Office again, I'm afraid. Apart from the usual crop of letters querying their bills, there is an absolutely irate one from Mr Chivers—Bernard Chivers who always has a suite here for Lords and does a lot of entertaining in the Restaurant."

"Yes, yes," said Andrew impatiently, "what next?"

"He was here in October for a week entertaining some American clients, bill of nearly a thousand pounds, and the Bill Office sent his account to a distant cousin."

Andrew rested his head in his hands in a gesture of despair.

"But that's not all. This is the second time they have done it. The first time the cousin just returned the bill to us; this time he sent it to Mr Bernard Chivers, with a tart comment that he was glad to see one member of the family could afford to spend a thousand pounds in a week while others had to exist on their pensions."

"This is disgraceful." Andrew looked at his watch, he was very angry. "Find out who is responsible and send him in at once. There is just time before the meeting."

"There is one other thing, Mr Merrin. The manager of the florist's shop keeps ringing to say some of their flowers have been stolen . . ."

"Rubbish," interrupted Andrew crossly, "they were needed for an emergency. The sooner we get rid of that shop the better. Mr Raffin knows all about it. Now, hurry up with the Bill Office, I want this sorted out first."

Robin Wearne, sauntering through the Front Hall to the Manager's Office, saw his mother by the Enquiry desk. She was wearing a grey suit with a white fur collar and cuffs, and as he approached he smelled the familiar breath of scent he remembered from childhood. She hadn't been a very attentive mother when he had been sick; it was nanny who had coped with all the unpleasant things, so that after the bowl of sickness had been removed, she would waft in smelling of distant scents that soothed and appealed.

"Is it alright to bring Patsy back this weekend?" he asked.

"Of course, darling, but I'll have to put off Tom and Nancy, unless he comes without her. I'll sort it all out when I get back—I'm just off to Paris."

"Lucky you," Robin, surprised, about to ask questions, was stopped by a wave of his mother's hand, expensively covered in grey kid.

"Should you be here?"

"Actually I'm on my way to the Manager's Office."

"Well, hurry darling, you know your grandfather's rule—never keep authority waiting."

In the outer office Merrin's secretary indicated the door marked Manager's Office.

"Go in, Mr Wearne," she said, "Mr Merrin is waiting for you."

Robin knocked, opened the door and smiled pleasantly. Might ask for a couple of hours off to see Patsy if all goes well, he thought, wondering why he had been summoned.

"Robin?" Andrew looked up, surprised. "Do you want something?"

"You sent for me," Robin, affable, shut the door, then felt the sudden hostility from behind the desk.

"Of course, I asked for the incompetent clerk in charge of bills sent on account, not realising it was you. No, don't sit down," he said, as Robin made a move for the chair, "I prefer you to stand."

Ten minutes later Robin found himself walking back through the outer office, past the secretary with head bent over her typewriter. He was very shaken. Alright, so he had made a mistake, and he had made it twice, but he wasn't going to be told he was useless to society by his godmother's husband, even if he was the hotel Manager.

Robin, pink-faced, knew why the secretary had hidden her face. The Chairman's son, working his way through the hotel, and taken apart for his inefficiency. It was embarrassing for him and for her; and Robin, flushed with anger, wanted to assert himself. Father, of course, was off chasing harmless animals in the fields of Hertfordshire, mother was off to Paris, godmother Charlotte, who had always shown the most understanding, would take Andrew's side. Patsy would understand, she always encouraged him. It was Patsy who had insisted he had a proper job and extolled the hotel industry. With uncle Robert as President, how could he fail? There were times when Robin, face to face with his own inadequacy, felt such a rage within him that he wanted to rush out in anger, causing harm and destruction and end in a blaze of glory. That's how one won the VC.

Now he walked slowly back to the Bill Office.

"Good officer material," they had said about him when he first joined the Army; "understands discipline and how to administer it."

Yes, discipline, the same in the hotel world as in the Army. He had made a balls of it, now he must sit and write a letter of apology and see it never happened again. And if it did, from one of the clerks under him, then, by God, would he give him hell. The thought calmed him.

'Understands discipline and how to administer it.'

Robin squared his shoulders and walked to his desk, not looking left or right, as if he had just been given a rise in salary. Perhaps, he thought, I might become a good hotelier. Same rules as the Army after all, but without the bullets.

NINE

"I'm glad you are not wearing a hat," Tom had said, "or perhaps they have all been bought up by the WI."

He'd smiled, holding out his hand. "I was in your father's regiment and this is a brother officer, Adrian Wearne."

Nancy had laughed, quick to catch his humour. There had been a Royal Garden party the day before for members of the Women's Institute— '9,000 hats—a milliner's dream' wrote the daily papers. Laughing had eased her tension standing outside St-Martin-in-the-Fields, shaking hands with her father's past friends and colleagues. She had felt very alone during the Memorial Service, in the predominantly male congregation, and had hoped not wearing a hat made her less conspicuous.

A few weeks later in Hatchards, lingering by the round table and admiring the shining circle of book jackets, she had heard a voice beside her:

"Hulloa. How nice to see you again. How are you coping without the General?"

The General, her father, had been a bad tempered, opinionated old man whom she had not mourned at all. She was sure Tom knew this and smiled, rather shyly.

"I'm a little lost," she paused, "after so long."

"After waiting on someone hand and foot for so long, you mean," said Tom, with an easy familiarity. He had looked at her short skirt with admiration, and Nancy had shrugged her shoulders in a sad, almost hopeless way.

"Come and have a drink at the pub," suggested Tom, "it's just round the corner."

The pub, the Regina, and the bar stool an upholstered chair in grey velvet.

"Nice pub," she had laughed as accolites appeared and she was offered champagne, plain, cocktail or Buck's Fizz.

"Buck's Fizz, I think. Father was a member of Bucks. Are you?" she added.

"Yes, as a matter of fact, but I only get there once or twice a month—this place is a club on its own."

It had been easy and pleasant together, as companionable as doing *The Times* crossword and both of them understanding the clues.

"What are you going to do with yourself?" Tom had asked, lighting her cigarette.

"I'd like to have a job," Nancy confided, "but there's really not much I can do except type and run a house."

"Do you need to?"

"Financially, no." Nancy put her down her glass, "but I rather feel I have been too long on my own."

"I wish we could have lunch." Tom bent to sign the bill, "but I have a columnist to entertain. He will either come wearing a better suit than mine and a silk tie, or slacks and a cardigan to show he is not impressed, in which case we shall be banished to the back of the Grill by Raymond."

Nancy remembered laughing, "I thought no one was allowed in without a suit."

"We have had to back pedal a bit, so many men, particularly Americans, wear those Rex Harrison cardigans now that we have to let them in. As long as they wear a tie, of course."

Tom, looking at her, neat in a dark suit with a shining cap of hair, added suddenly:

"I have a suggestion to make. There are two young girls in my office, full of ideas and loyalty, God bless them, but a bit inclined to put Mr Fred Smith Esq., on an envelope, and they haven't the faintest idea that the daughter of an Earl is the Lady Hilaria of what have you by right." Tom shrugged his shoulders. "And whatever one might feel in this day and age, like Debrett, people do expect us to get it right, and we have had one or two caustic remarks lately. How would you like to run the office for me? Can you have dinner tonight and talk about it?"

How many years ago? Nancy, standing in the empty office, looked at Tom's desk and wondered where he was. Last night he had suggested a night cap together but had not turned up and she had spent a fretful night, the central heating turned to seventy degrees for American clients, had left her limp, her usually bright hair had a tired flatness, and the shadows under her eyes gave a bruised look.

There was a small oval looking-glass on the end wall, it was in a poor light and Tom hated it.

"Do get rid of that damn thing, it sneers at me," he had said, turning away from it. "No matter how well I feel it always makes me look as if I had just been dug up."

Exactly how I look. Dispirited, Nancy walked over to her desk and picked up the telephone to ask for the Works Department. Today was definitely the day to get rid of that offending glass. She had high hopes that this Monday might have been a special day, that last night Tom would at last have talked of marriage. And if he had, she would have accepted. Nancy, at thirty-eight, wanted a husband and a home and children. There was still time, she told herself, but it was getting late in the day. She liked Tom, she liked his life-style and they were friends. That was a good enough basis for marriage in the Victorian tradition, a tradition of which she approved. Duty and obeying the rules, but no nonsense about passionate love, something which Nancy had never known and of which she was afraid. As Tom is too, she thought, I'm sure he is; it's why we have this rapport together without having to talk about it.

"Darling," sang Louise, bursting into the office; "just two things—I don't want to disturb you when I know how busy you are." Her quick eyes took in the empty office and there was a mischievous smile, fair hair falling on to the soft fur collar, the inevitable breath of Arpège.

"First, just a hint of crisis about next weekend, as Robin wants to bring Patsy back from the hospital. I'm not exactly sending off victory fireworks but I must try and be a good mum. Would it be alright if you just came for the day on Sunday?"

What she means, thought Nancy angrily, is that if I shared Tom's bed there would be room for us both.

"Ask them to ring back," she said, and put down the receiver. "Not to worry," she turned to Louise, and added crisply, "and what's the other thing?"

"The new hotel Jeudwine is buying in Paris—do you know where it is? Our revered President didn't think much of his suite here, that I should have a look at pastures new and get some ideas."

Louise perched on Tom's desk, swinging her legs.

"Where's Tom?" she asked. "Hasn't he surfaced yet?"

"He was up late."

"Weren't we all?" Louise shrugged slim shoulders. "I even went down to the Front Hall in the early hours to get the papers—rather disappointing." She took a quick look at Nancy in case Tom should mention their meeting by the lift.

"The Hotel Josephine is off the Rue d'Astorg—I'll get the number for you."

Nancy walked into the outer office, uneasy, fearing the glow that surrounded Louise; sensual, as if she had just got out of bed and was showing her naked body with pride. Abrasive, she rubs my nerves with gravel Nancy said to herself, and she always will.

Madeleine, plain round face flushed with animation, was bent over a newspaper spread across the nearest desk.

"We're on the front page!" she shouted. "Isn't it wonderful."

There was Mr Bertioni, an elegant finger pointing at the cake, his face one of great pleasure, and in the fuzzy background, the ghost of a chef's hat.

For a moment Nancy forgot Louise.

"Oh, that is really good. Order lots of copies . . ."

"May I see?"

Louise had followed, and now exclaimed extravagantly.

"Clever girls," she said, waving a pretty hand to Madeleine and Dorothy. "I shall never call you Mad and Dotty again!"

They giggled happily. Madeleine, the larger of the two, answered the telephone, her fond eyes still on Louise.

"It's the Manager's Office again about the flowers . . ."

"Now do be sure to order lots of copies," Louise looked earnest, "before they put this picture on an inside page or leave it out altogether in the next edition."

"Yes, Lady Wearne." Dorothy, thin, fair hair looped across her face, eagerly rushed to the door. "I'll go down to the Enquiry Office right away."

Nancy promised to ring back when Tom arrived. No, she didn't know about the flowers; yes, he was somewhere in the building, they were very busy; yes, she would ring back as soon as she could . . . all the time her eyes were on Louise, charming the staid Madeleine into undreamed of animation.

"Save me as many copies as you can spare, my dear. I must fly. 'Bye Nancy."

"Why is it that Louise always gets away with murder?" she'd asked Tom angrily. They were driving back from the weekend in Hertfordshire and Nancy had been stiff with frustration and inhibitions.

"I feel as if I am caught in a wire mesh, struggling." Knowing she was being cross, complaining, doing all the things Tom hated, yet she could not stop.

"Louise is years older than I am, it's time she stopped behaving in such a—such a—" she had hesitated, not finding the words she wanted, "in such a young way," she had finished lamely.

"Light me a cigarette," said Tom, eyes straight ahead watching for unexpected walkers in the unlit country lane. He knew every turn, but Nancy was distracting him with her whining.

"Louise behaves in such a young way, as you say," said

Tom, inhaling deeply, "because she never thinks about age. She is also blessed with youthful looks and figure and, most important of all," Tom took his eyes off the road for a second and glanced into the darkness at Nancy, "she doesn't brood."

"What does that mean?" asked Nancy, instantly on the defensive.

"It means," said Tom, "that she is one of those fortunate people who can live in the present—in now—without any backward looks of regret and no forward looks of envy."

Now the anger and frustration were there again—the depths of misery she had known in the dark landscape when Tom had braked suddenly to avoid a cat pouncing into the grassy hedge. She had fallen forward and knocked her head, not badly but at once all her fears and anger had broken like a boil in a moment of unheralded fright.

She had made the most of it, tears, fuss, and the slight hurt from the impact had gone before her anger.

They had driven back in silence and Tom had left her at her flat with:

"Take the morning off. You may have concussion."

He had driven away without a backward glance and Nancy hated Louise with an intensity that was deeper than any feeling she had ever experienced.

She had lost her way, and she knew it. From the very first she had not understood the relationship. Tom and Adrian had been at school together, chaps in the Regiment together, and when Tom had joined the Regina, at Adrian's suggestion, he had gone to live with them. But Louise seemed to be above it all. She tolerated Tom, she tolerated Adrian and to a degree she tolerated her son, Robin. So what was the adrenalin that kept her so in love with life?

They had a Georgian house in Hertfordshire with an ancient retainer who sat in the kitchen shelling peas or peeling potatoes and demanding news of Mr Robin. There was a maid and a gardener but Louise did all the cooking; expertly, carelessly and always as if she was far away thinking of something else.

"You're looking very peaky," Tom said, breezing through the door, looking at Nancy with a critical eye; "and you should be on top of the world—front page!"

"The Manager's Office want to know about some flowers," said Nancy stiffly, "they've been on and on ..."

"Oh, bugger them," said Tom cheerfully, "they were for Alicia Berger, who is quite enchanting, by the way, and I think we should really go to town on the photo call ..."

"I thought she wasn't arriving until today,"

"Well, she arrived in the middle of the night with no shoes on—but old Spiros and I coped. I'll tell you over a glass of champagne—you look as if you need it. Hold the fort, Mad—you know where we'll be."

"Morning, Charlie," Tom rested an elbow on the bar, "Two champagne cocktails, I think a little booster is needed." He glanced at Nancy with a sympathetic smile.

"Cheer up," he said. "Plenty of brandy in it, Charlie."

"It's the sugar that brings out the alcohol." Charlie, an elderly Puck, thin, merry face and a fluff of white hair, dropped a sugar lump into each glass.

"Well we need more than sugar today," said Tom amiably. "How did you enjoy the party?"

Charlie topped the glasses up with champagne, added a slice of orange and passed them across the bar in what seemed almost one movement.

For a moment the humorous face became still.

"You know, Mr Raffin, I think it was one of the best evenings I have ever had. I've been here nearly forty years now, part of the furniture you might say, and I don't remember enjoying myself so much. Seeing all the old faces, worn very well they had, men particularly. But then men wear better than women ... No disrespect to you, Miss," he exclaimed hastily to Nancy, his old face animated with fine lines, "you're one of the lucky ones, good bones, slim as a bean pole, it's the plump ones who have to worry. Do you remember that blonde Swedish star who came over to take the lead in the spy film—can't remember the name. Same again, Sir?"

"Anastasia, or something like that?"

"That's it, first time here and Tony Desmond had to meet her. Got here first and some state he was in. I remember I gave him a whisky sour and he had to hold the glass in two hands to get it to his mouth. After he'd had a second one he stopped trembling so much and then I saw her coming in—well, you couldn't miss her"

Charlie slid two more glasses across, "Black dress she'd been poured into—Tony's eyes nearly popped out of his head—well, so did mine," he laughed with a wry look at Nancy, who said crisply:

"No orange in mine, please."

"Certainly, madam."

Charlie removed her glass and Tom turned crossly.

"Oh, don't interrupt, Nancy. Go on Charlie, what happened?"

"Well, they sat down in one of the alcoves, she had a passion fruit cocktail and he had another whisky sour and they seemed to be getting on well ... she was laughing a lot and bending forward to hear what he said. And then suddenly she looked rather coy, I couldn't hear what she said, but she indicated the back of her dress, and Tony got up, looking very embarrassed, and tried to do up her zip which had obviously come undone, but his hands were shaking so much I doubt if he could have shut a door, let alone fasten a zip. So then she gave an impatient toss of her head and came over to me:

"'Do up my dress, barman,' she said.

"Starkers she was, under that dress, and it was open right down to her—beg your pardon, Miss," at Nancy's stiff face—"right down below her backbone, as you might say."

Tom was laughing, looking young and relaxed. Nancy, watching him, feeling vaguely hostile and wishing she had not worn her brown suit which did nothing for her and always made her feel as if she was doing penance, knew she was being dreary and could do nothing about it. Even the champagne could not ease her depression.

Tom was now laughing uproariously.

"Then what?" he asked.

"Oh, well they went off together and there was quite a union for a time, but she couldn't stop eating and he couldn't stop drinking and the last time she came in here, years later, if she'd asked me to do up her dress I'd have needed a bib and tackle."

"Your office on the telephone, Miss," said a waiter at her elbow, and Nancy followed him to the telephone set on a shelf against the Regency striped wall.

"Miss Berger has just telephoned," said Madeleine, "she wants . . ."

"Miss Who?" interrupted Nancy sharply.

"Alicia Berger." Madeleine sounded excited. "She wants Mr Raffin to go up straight away—she sounded awfully sweet."

"Alicia Berger wants to see you," said Nancy, returning to the bar, "I'm going back to the office."

"Alicia Berger, ah, I remember her," said Charlie, collecting the empty glasses, "Pretty little thing, appealing, I suppose you might say, small and needed looking after. I went to her first show, she didn't stay here, but she came in once or twice. Didn't think much of her manager, using her as they all do, and as they all do, I think she married him. I wonder what she looks like now?"

"She looks—well, as you said, Charlie—appealing. I'll bring her in to see you before she goes."

Appealing, yes. Alicia opened the door wearing something long, soft and pale blue. There were ruffles round the neck and her hair was tied back with a blue satin ribbon.

"I'm having brunch," she said, "bacon and eggs and orange juice, but I've got champagne on ice for you and some smoked salmon sandwiches in case you skipped breakfast."

"Genius, pure genius," Tom helped himself. "I did skip breakfast and now I shall skip lunch and stay and imbibe with

109

you. I might even pour some champagne into your orange juice and give you a Buck's Fizz."

"Is that good?"

Tom, struggling with the wire round the top of the bottle turned and smiled.

"Very," he said, and eased the cork out gently.

"Oh, it didn't pop."

"It shouldn't," Tom filled his glass quickly. "If it does, it is too warm and it is a vulgar noise if you are sitting at the next table and only drinking lager."

Alicia laughed. "Hotel lore?" She held out her glass. "Too much orange juice?"

"No, about right." Tom handed back her glass, then raised his own.

"To you."

The pansy brown eyes looked softer with no mascara, and her skin had that clean look which either meant no make up or something expensive cleverly applied. I wouldn't know, thought Tom, but the effect was fresh and pleasing.

"You look very young," he added.

Alicia bent forward and kissed him lightly. Her scent was discreet and flowery.

"You always make me feel good," she said, and immediately moved far away from him and sat in an armchair by the window.

"Thank you for sending the cable," she said, "The boys called me this morning, they are on their way." She sighed. "So this is my last little time of freedom."

Tom ate two sandwiches in quick succession.

"My favourite blotting paper," he smiled, refilling his glass. He held the bottle high, looking at her, raising a dark eyebrow enquiringly.

"Sure," Alicia answered, "it makes me feel good."

"Are you still married to the manager of yours?" asked Tom, perching on the arm of her chair.

She looked surprised.

"Oh, you knew about that, then. It was over years ago, but

110

we sort of hung on. He's awfully dull and boring and talks about money all day long, and he isn't even pretty." Alicia put her head on one side, giving Tom an appraising look, "Like you."

Tom raised his glass, giving a mock bow in acknowledgement. He felt quite extraordinarily well.

"Go on," he said.

"Well, nothing really—that's just it—nothingness." She sighed. "He doesn't shave in the morning and wears awful tee shirts that are too tight and have crude mottoes. Not much of a compliment to me."

Alicia bent forward to arrange a fold of chiffon round her slim legs.

"I like to be made to feel good, and when I go out on stage I need to feel the audience is wanting me. Do you understand?" She looked up, uncertain.

"Of course." Tom smiled and came over to sit beside her, touching her hand.

Alicia continued as if she had not noticed.

"Then I finally insisted on a divorce—at least it meant we didn't have to share a bed when we went on tour."

She laughed suddenly, almost shyly, "Now I have one bedroom to myself and the boys can share the other one."

"I'd forgotten you had a double suite. Which room did you choose?"

"The best one, naturally. The one with the pink drapes."

Alicia stood up, stretching.

"Want to have a look?" she asked casually, not looking at Tom, who at once put down his glass and followed her. He had known it would end like this since their first drink together last night. It was a pleasant feeling, a mixture of excitement and apprehension. He looked back into the sitting room and saw the tired pink roses.

"I must send you some fresh flowers," he said, closing the bedroom door behind him.

"Tom Raffin has completely disappeared," said Andrew.

111

"What have you ordered for lunch, I haven't much time?"

"Fish," replied Charlotte, handing him a glass of champagne, "in lots of creamy sauce and masses of plain boiled potatoes to mop it up, and if that doesn't fatten you up, I'll despair."

"God, I needed that." Andrew stood up. "Better have lunch straight away—can't spare long."

Charlotte pushed him gently back into his chair.

"I've ordered it for a quarter past one, which will give you ten minutes to relax and enjoy a drink. What do you mean about Tom? Doesn't Nancy Thing know?"

"Nancy Thing, as you and Louise call her, and I wish you wouldn't as I'm going to do the same one day, is very sour and evasive—'am I my brother's keeper?' and all that kind of stuff. I've got two problems I want to clear up with him and be done with it." Andrew smiled across at Charlotte.

"Now you've Delilahed me into this stuff you might at least keep my glass replenished. It's almost given me enough spirit to fire that damn little Belgian in the Grill."

"Is that a good idea?"

"In that he is incompetent, idle, arrogant and does not have the respect of his staff, the answer is 'yes'. But taking into account that the Union would almost certainly call a strike claiming unfair dismissal, victimisation, you name it, then the answer is definitely 'no'. We just can't afford strikes in time or money."

Charlotte sipped champagne and nibbled an olive, looking into the distance.

"Why don't you kick him upstairs?" she asked.

"I know where I'd like to kick him," Andrew replied with irritation, "That remark's not up to your usual standards."

"No, I mean it," Charlotte continued placidly. "Why not put him on the floors—put him in charge of old whatshisname, who's due to retire anyway, or so I'm told. If he's only number two or three in the Grill and is made number one—head waiter for all floors—surely that's a kick upstairs and it will also get rid of him from the front of the theatre."

112

"Darling child," said Andrew, tired lines smoothed by a warm smile. "What would I do without you? You have the germ of a very good idea. I'll talk to Bertioni about it this afternoon."

"How is the birthday boy today?"

Charlotte, feeling lightheaded with happiness, bent to kiss the top of Andrew's head. It was all she wanted from life, to be able to listen and to help, to smooth even one wrinkle from that dear tired face by just being there.

"You can have your lunch now," she smiled pressing the bell marked Floor Waiter. "You didn't answer my question."

"Bertioni? He's been clossetted with our President all the morning, but I did see him before nine o'clock, standing at the top of the stairs and gazing down at his world with such an expression of contentment on his face that I crept past without even saying 'Good Morning'."

TEN

Bertioni had indeed been aware of Merrin quietly passing behind him as he stood at the head of the stairs and had been grateful for his silence. He had not wanted to be involved in conventional pleasantries at that moment, but to be left on the bridge of his ship in command; and in command of his own, to think his own thoughts and to savour all the subtle flavours of the previous evening. The clock, Lobb's speech, Miss Ballater's violets, all the old familiar faces, the hard hand shakes as if by their hardness they conveyed the strength of their feelings. It was a tapestry that had been stitched slowly and carefully over the years, not to be stored in a dark cupboard of memory, but to be looked at and loved every day.

For a while Bertioni permitted himself the luxury of standing, reflecting, and letting his mind drift . . .

> *What is this life, if full of care*
> *We have no time to stand and stare?*

Louise's favourite poem as a small girl, though she could never remember what came next. "Streams full of stars", she would recite, then look up at him with that beguiling smile, "can't remember." And he would get her book and coach her for the lessons tomorrow. Little blonde elphin girl, who had grown too quickly and danced away. When the poet had died in 1940 he had handed her *The Times* across the breakfast table.

"W.H. Davies? Was he my favourite poet?" she had laughed, pouring more coffee. "It's Swinburne now," and she had left the paper unread.

Little vignettes of Louise flitting like fireflies; yet Paul, his only son, was always in the shadows, barely visible. The news of his death had numbed him, but to Beryl it had been a desolation, a waste which stretched on and on with no respite. She had never recovered, neither had she wanted to, wearing her grief like a shield and daring him to touch it.

Il passato è passato, Bertioni said to himself, stroking the smooth surface of his cigarette case, what is past is past. But of course it never is, for once he questioned his familiar motto.

"It is not going to be an easy job steering the Regina through the next decade," Sir John had said. "Easier to keep up standards, discipline, when there's an enemy to fight." They had been drinking champagne together to celebrate victory and his voice had been tired. "I don't envy you Mr Bertioni, I don't envy you."

He had been right, of course. After the war the sense of purpose disappeared overnight. Food rationing became stricter, dreary day followed dreary day with nothing to look forward to—they, the victors, were the vanquished; and beaten Germany, financed by America, worked hard and grew prosperous. It had been hard to take and morale had been very low. Worst of all was the pilfering.

"It's got to stop," Adrian Wearne had said. He was very much the new Chairman, sitting in the winged chair in his office and waving Bertioni to the chair opposite him.

"Apart from the food which disappears, which is appalling, there is never any soap in the cloakrooms and upstairs is worst of all. I've just had a scathing letter from Mr Jeudwine about those friends of his from Illinois. Apparently the wife lost several pairs of nylons and some of her underwear. That's no way to get business."

"Spoils of war," Bertioni had said, feeling for his cigarette case, then remembering where he was.

"Meaning," said Adrian, "that we haven't had any?"

"Exactly." Bertioni had looked across at the creased pink face with its uncertain contours, the weak mouth, and the surprisingly light thick eyelashes.

115

"Don't'tell me you of all people are condoning it?" Adrian opened the cigarette box in front of him and pushed it across the desk. "Help yourself."

Bertioni inhaled gratefully. A little less of the Chairman and a dash of the son-in-law. He smiled a trifle wryly.

"Of course not," he'd said, "but I do understand, and understanding is half the battle. What we need is a strong Staff Manager. I have been thinking about it for some time . . ."

"Better to have their handbags searched when they leave the staff entrance," Adrian had interrupted.

"That would be fatal," Bertioni was outraged. "When you have fought for your country, lost possessions, perhaps your home, you don't expect to be treated like a common criminal —for every one who *had* stolen something there would remain twenty innocent and very offended other staff."

"Alright then," Adrian had sighed, getting up and pouring sherry from the crystal decanter on the table behind his desk. "I thought this was going to be a friendly . . ." he'd stopped and handed Bertioni a glass. "At least we might as well have a drink if we are going to argue."

"It's quite simple." In command, Bertioni was brief, he'd realised his son-in-law was already bored. "Salter—Major Salter, would be ideal as Staff Manager. I remember your uncle saying that when he came back, with his record, he would not like going back to the Enquiry Office. We made him Manager, as you know, but he still feels subservient. He needs to deal with men, not hand out keys and information."

"And the present Staff Manager?"

"I'll change him over to the Enquiry Office—he's very subservient, which is why he can't control the staff." Bertioni put out his cigarette with his usual neatness and stood up.

"I'll go ahead then," he'd said, without waiting for a reply. He knew how to handle Adrian with his low threshold of boredom; but Louise, did she know how, with her quick silver mind, her capacity for loving? Why had she chosen Adrian, he had wondered, as he walked away along the corridor. It was then he had seen the worn patch of carpet by the lift and his

116

mind had switched at once to its replacement and the Works Department.

Salter had been a success as Staff Manager.

"If you can get through Anzio, you can get through this lot," he had greeted his new appointment cheerfully. He had brought back a kindly discipline, no bags were searched, but loyalty and honesty were appealed to as something worthwhile, and the pilfering had stopped.

As time went by he had been promoted to Assistant General Manager, and now Bertioni watched him make his way across the Front Hall. A van driver had brought in a stack of newspapers and had already stayed too long gossiping over the Enquiry Office counter, a fact noticed by Bertioni and also by Salter, who walked importantly to the counter and the van driver disappeared.

Bertioni made his way slowly down the staircase, knowing that Salter had seen him too and would be there to greet him.

"Good morning, Sir. What a splendid gathering last night. I trust you enjoyed it as much as we all did?"

Straight shoulders, ramrod back, carefully waved hair and a small neat moustache. A little plumper now, the folds of his morning jacket carefully tailored. Bertioni had a sudden vision of the old Reception Manager, Feraud, small, plump, but beautifully camouflaged and with a wicked eye. Salter was orthodox and Army, and he was respected, one didn't get a decoration at Anzio for nothing.

"I enjoyed it so much," smiled Bertioni, "that I have had to put my enjoyment away in a drawer for the moment, otherwise I shall do no work at all. But I shall bring it out many times to look at and remember."

Salter felt a slight unease. The old boy was never poetic and he was not sure of the correct response, but Bertioni continued, after a long look at the Enquiry Office.

"I would like your opinion. It seemed to me, looking down, from my perch—" here he smiled "as I know you all refer to it, it seemed to me that the Front Hall has become very much like a railway station, lots of people waiting,

117

hanging about but nothing to attract their attention while so doing. I am hopeful of having our own Florist Department again, open until quite late so that carnations and little posies can be bought as in the old days. I would also like to have our own bookstall again, but that may have to wait. This dreary counter," Bertioni led the way to a display of airline and holiday folders, "with no one behind it to even give advice is a waste of valuable space. I thought this would be the ideal place for our florist, but then where would we have the bookstall? I must go, I am seeing the President at ten, but he will want to know just where I want to put everything. Will you think about it for me?"

Wily old bugger, he knows exactly where he is going to put everything but he wants us all to be involved. Salter stood upright, and of course we are, we love the bloody place and we love him.

Escorting Bertioni to the lift, Salter pressed the button for the correct floor, and said, lifting his chin and looking straight ahead.

"May I suggest, Sir, that you take the President to the Restaurant for luncheon instead of the Grill?"

"Why?" at once Bertioni was alert.

"There has been a slight disturbance in the Grill kitchens, nothing to worry about, Mr Merrin has it all under control." Watching the light flickering down to the ground floor, Salter saw the lift doors open. "Just a suggestion, Sir," he said, standing to one side as two passengers walked past.

Already a light flashed on an upstairs floor and Bertioni knew the doors would begin to close. Oh, for old Arthur, sitting on a stool with his jaundiced view of life; his manners were impeccable, never would the doors have closed while a conversation was in progress.

"Very well," he said, through the half-closed doors, meaning to add, "and make the necessary arrangements," but he was already ascending, and almost immediately stopped at the second floor.

Outside the President's suite, the valet waited, key in hand.

"Good morning, Sir," he said, giving a light knock and opening the door at the same time.

"Ah, Carlo, good morning, I have some fresh coffee for you. Milk, cream, sugar?" Silver grey suit, very pale with a lot of white silk cuff showing, cuff links the size of gold nuggets —and probably are—Bertioni took in the man and the room in one sharp glance.

"Black, please," he said, "and no sugar."

"What, at this time in the morning?" Jeudwine gave one of his practised smiles. "Don't tell me our revered Managing Director has a hangover?"

"Certainly not." Bertioni produced his silver case. "May I?" he asked, and, barely waiting for the answering nod, he lit a cigarette, inhaled, and continued: "I always drink black coffee, at any and every time of the day and night, it is the only way . . ." and here he made a graceful gesture, cigarette between his long thin fingers, "I know the coffee is up to standard, strong and freshly ground—anything else can mask the flavour."

He threw a quizzical glance at Jeudwine lighting a fat cigar. And I wouldn't do that at ten o'clock in the morning, and if I was forced to, I'd remove the band. His eyes, always watchful, noticed the black velvet mocassins piped in gold braid, and rested there.

"Don't worry." Jeudwine, following Bertioni's gaze, laughed. "I'm not waiting for my shoes to be cleaned—they were here at eight o'clock. In fact, they were so goddam clean that I haven't dared put them on yet."

Bertioni lifted his hand, as if in salute. "I think we understand each other," he said.

"Well, I understand you want to have a florist's department again and have your own bookstall, and I'm ready to agree to both as long as we make a profit."

"We always did in the past."

"Did we? Why did we change then?"

119

Bertioni paused, then said carefully, "New broom perhaps?"

"Hardly new, we've owned the Regina since about 1945 or thereabouts, and I've still never managed to mould it into the Lincoln Hotels complex." Jeudwine looked straight across at Bertioni. "With a little help from my friends," he added.

Bertioni smiled, shrugged his shoulders, and carefully tapped ash from his cigarette.

"New ideas have to be tried, but sometimes they don't work out and then we should go back to the precepts which did, or at least give them another try while we think again. I believe the Regina has a part to play in the hotel world by being old fashioned—there are quite a lot of old-fashioned people about still, and they may only make one visit a year, but they dream about it and remember it with pleasure for all those months; at least I hope they remember it with pleasure, because if they don't, it is our fault."

Jeudwine stubbed out his cigar, not very well, and there was a stale aroma which Bertioni found distasteful, watching the smouldering, sodden, unravelling ends. He heard Jeudwine at the telephone saying "Waiter, I am ready now," and walked across to the window, his back to the room.

Almost immediately his trained ear heard the waiter's tap on the door, the well-remembered trundle of the white-linened table. Turning, he saw the two glasses of champagne, the glass bowl of potato chips—*not* chips with champagne, he thought, and the irritated flick of his hand sent a message. At once ash trays, smouldering cigar ends were removed and the waiter returned to hand Bertioni a glass with an anxious upturned glance. Bertioni nodded and smiled.

"A little celebration," said Jeudwine, taking the glass offered him and waving away the waiter in the same grand gesture. "A little celebration because we are both professionals."

If you were a pro, Bertioni smiled to himself, you would have ordered a bottle, and with a good label. As it was he smiled, raised his glass and listened.

"I was at a party at the White House recently," Jeudwine

said, settling himself back on the sofa, making the sort of airy gesture which meant he was not trying to be upstage, but it just happened to be a fact of life that he was invited to the White House; and Bertioni, recognising this, nodded and looked with attention.

"I was introduced to a Senator's wife as the President of Lincoln Hotels, and do you know what she said? 'Why, that's wonderful, that means you own that darling little Regina Hotel in London—it's my most favourite hotel in the whole world'."

Bertioni laughed. He was pleased and the hard planes of his face seemed to soften, as if light had played across them.

"That's very handsome of you," he said, "and very honest."

"I'm an honest man," replied Jeudwine, putting down his glass and looking across at Bertioni, his dark eyes deep, unfathomable, no ripple across the surface, "which is what I am going to be now. I want you to have Jan back here."

"Jan?" Bertioni took out his cigarette case, "Oh, of course, Vitold." He picked up the small square of purple Regina matches beside him, lit his cigarette and inhaled to cover his alertness.

"Why?" he asked.

"Because I'm being really honest now," Jeudwine smiled with his mouth but not his eyes, "Jan has outlived his usefulness to me. He has a good financial brain, is loyal and, what is it you say over here?—sea green incorruptible, whatever that might mean, but I guess it means he doesn't take bribes."

"So why . . .?" began Bertioni.

"He is old hat, that's why. He does everything he is told, never lets me down, but I can't rid him of that middle European habit of living in the past—he just doesn't fit in with this century."

"It's taken you a long time to find out," replied Bertioni mildly, then regretted it, seeing Jeudwine stiffen as he looked down at his wrist, fiddling with the gold chain bracelet.

"I didn't want to order you," he said, "I would just like

you to accept it as a good idea, that you should take on Jan here at the Regina."

Bertioni had a feeling of unease, of suspicion, and inhaling deeply from his cigarette, tapped it out neatly, half smoked, into the green glass ashtray beside him. Aware that Jeudwine was watching him, he took his time.

"What you are saying," he said with a slight smile, "is that as we are an old-fashioned hotel, Vitold will fit in very well. But in what capacity?"

"As your assistant."

"I don't need an assistant." Bertioni felt a wave of great distress, his manhood, his ability, his whole zest for life were being questioned and no one had ever questioned them before.

"Not now." Jeudwine was smooth, seeing the tight lips and narrowed eyes. "You are younger than all of us, Carlo, and I expect you to go on as you are for years . . ." an expansive smile—"for decades to come. But one must have someone to take over eventually. I, myself, am doing just that, taking my young nephew straight from Yale and training him to follow in my footsteps. I like young . . ." he was about to say people but stopped, waving his hand and saying quickly instead, "ideas, young ideas. Young ideas from my side of the Atlantic and you keep your cherished old ones here. That is why I want you to do me a favour, Carlo, and take on Jan. You will like him."

"I already do," replied Bertioni stiffly, "but is he going to approve such a change?"

"He will if you put it to him as your idea, that he is your choice and that you intend to approach me about it. That way it won't look as if I'm getting rid of him."

Jeudwine stood up. "Well, I mustn't keep you, I know how busy you are. I shall look forward to lunching with you when we can talk about interior decorating. I find this room very dull."

"Which was what you were meant to do." Stressed, Bertioni spoke without his usual caution, then added quickly, with one of his most polished smiles, a slight shrug of his shoulders: "Now, perhaps we can look forward to a little loosening of the purse strings to include some new furnishings?"

The pause which followed proved to Bertioni, which his senses had told him already, that he had gone too far. Robert Jeudwine was the President of the Regina, the boss who held the purse strings, an American Jew with deeply felt inhibitions, who had been made to feel suddenly that he had lost control, and Bertioni, contrite, and a little afraid, said quickly:

"Louise was very distressed that you had been given this suite. She has just finished the third and fourth floors and wanted you to see them. And now, hearing of your feelings, she is off to Paris today." Bertioni said and repeated it, "Today, to find something—" he was about to say worthy and stopped. "Something she thought would please you."

"Well, she had better postpone her trip to Paris and have lunch with us." Jeudwine walked to the door and held it open. "We have a lot to discuss."

A red light flicked red at the end of the passage, and Bertioni, disturbed as he was, noticed it at once and forgot for a moment that he was too old and should have a deputy, that he had not behaved with his usual immaculate control. He walked at once towards the dispense kitchen at the end of the corridor.

To his relief, a waiter hurried round the corner, menu in hand, knocked at the door, then opened it with his pass-key.

Bertioni, unnoticed, standing silently, watched, then walked away round the corner to the lift and pressed the button.

He was aware of great depression. Suddenly, all the things he had not wanted to know, to think about, had been presented to him in the full glare of spotlights. He was 75 years old. He might look and feel twenty years younger but the system said that 75 was old, so he was old and he was mortal.

"Death, in itself is nothing; but we fear . . ." a line remembered from something read long ago—he could not remember where or when, but it had etched into his memory and frightened him, "To be we know not what, we know not where."

Death had to be here, at the Regina, falling asleep, perhaps, upstairs, with all well around him. Bertioni walked into the Front Hall and saw Louise sitting in one of the sofas, quietly elegant, not moving.

Seeing him, her face became alive.

"I've been waiting and waiting—do tell. How did it go?"

Bertioni sat down beside her.

"All is well," he said, loving her, "and we have not only the flowers back again but the newspapers as well."

"But you don't look—you don't look . . ." Louise fumbled for words, her eyes anxious, "you don't look as happy as you should, as I would hope you to look. I've jolly nearly missed my plane waiting for you, so please be happy."

"I am, my dear, but I have to give something in return."

"Something you don't like?"

"No."

"Then something you don't approve of?"

"Not exactly." Bertioni stood up. "Jeudwine wants you to lunch with us to talk about the interior decorating so we will have to cancel your flight. I'll get the Enquiry Office to do it for you and book you another one this afternoon."

Louise watched him cross the foyer and saw the porters straighten their shoulders, the clerks behind the Enquiry desk alert and waiting, pageboys at attention, stiff as waxworks. What a presence he has, something indefinable but dominant. Without him, the whole hotel would collapse like a pack of cards, and would I collapse too, she wondered idly, smoothing the soft kid of her gloved hand. If I did not have it all behind me—tickets booked, cars at the door, everything paid for and organised . . .

"It's all taken care of," Bertioni was back, looking down at her, "and I've left a message for Vitold that he is to meet you. Can't have you arriving in Paris in the dark on your own."

Louise's smile was wistful. Even that. Even one's lover instructed to be there. She wondered how her father would react if he knew and pushed the thought from her quickly.

"Caesar's wife must be above suspicion . . ." The never-to-be-forgotten words. Years ago he had said them to her, when old Sir John had died and Adrian had become Chairman. And yet, this morning, the waiter opening the door for her, she had slipped in and stood behind him as he watched his clock strike nine, and told him she was going to Paris to see the satin and velvet draperies at the Josephine before they disappeared for ever under the Lincoln Hotel axe. And he had been pleased and trusting, glad that Vitold had made the suggestion and would be there to look after her. Now she stood up and put her hand on Bertioni's arm. "I wish you were coming to Paris with me," she said, adding, "You look just as young now as you did then."

By the softness in his eyes as he watched her, Louise knew she had pleased him. For some reason, she had pleased him more than she knew or understood. How many years ago and still as fresh, that time they had together after the war. He had bought her a silver chain—and I haven't worn it for ages, Louise contrite, searched her memory. It's upstairs in my jewel box—I'll wear it for lunch—my black dress, as I'm arriving in the evening, not this suit.

"There's Miss Ballater," she said, seeing the hesitant figure in the dark suit, lavender silk scarf, carefully upswept hair. "Looking for you?"

"Yeah, Yeah, Yeah," shouted the Beatles, as Miss Ballater pushed open the pub door. There were other sounds, all loud, as she looked past the fruit machines, to the old corner table. Moxon was there, looking towards the door, and seeing her, his face relaxed and he stood up, smiling.

"How did it go?" he asked, pulling out her chair. "Not the old pub we knew," he apologised, indicating the gin and tonic he had ordered for her, "but times have a nasty habit of changing."

"Not for us," Miss Ballater touched Moxon's hand shyly. "I'm going to run the Florist department again—I'm so happy I can hardly speak." Then, confused, she removed her hand and picked up her glass.

"To you," said Moxon, raising his beer glass, "and to us and to the Regina."

They smiled at each other.

"How will you get there? Covent Garden is such a long way now."

"Mr Bertioni didn't want me to go to the market, just to supervise back at the Regina; but of course, I explained that buying the flowers is the beginning and the end . . ."

"The Alpha and Omega," smiled Moxon and Miss Ballater nodded and hurried on. "I'm to have a driver and a small van and, best of all, I am to have a room on the top floor. To tell you the truth," she confided, "I'm awfully tired of living with my sister—she is so social."

"Alright if we sit here, Ma?" Leather jacket, mane of crimped hair, crisp packet thrown on the table.

"OK, Kev, room 'ere."

There was a scraping of chairs pulled back, the sudden smell of worn clothes, worked, played and probably slept in.

Moxon finished his beer and prepared to leave.

"We're just going," he said pleasantly, taking Miss Ballater's arm.

"Don't want to drive you away, Dad."

The laughter followed them to the door.

"Not our pub any more," Moxon was apologetic. "Though I sometimes wonder how they made it pay in the old days—just you and I and perhaps half a dozen others . . ."

"And that fat tabby in the best seat by the fire . . ."

"I'll find us another one like it." Moxon held her arm as they stood on the corner of the quiet street off Piccadilly. "And now we're going to eat roast beef at Simpson's."

"Well, that won't have changed," said Miss Ballater comfortably, "look, there's a taxi." She waved an imperious arm as the taxi passed without slackening pace.

"Only one way," Moxon put his hand to his mouth and gave a piercing whistle. At once the taxi slowed, made a U turn and drew up beside them.

126

"Ulloa, Guv. Know that sound anywhere. How's retirement then?"

Moxon shook the hand offered him through the open window, an old hand in knitted brown mittens with oil-encrusted nails.

"I'm thinking of going back," he confided.

"You all do," the elderly driver adjusted the meter. "You all go back, and once there you'll stay until you leave in your box." He laughed, wiping his nose against the back of his hand, and Moxon laughed with him.

"Worse things could happen."

"Sure thing—where to, Guv?"

"Simpson's." Stepping into the taxi Moxon looked across at his companion, wary of disapproval, but Miss Ballater, bright patches of colour high on her cheekbones, relaxed and animated, smiled reassuringly.

"That was quite splendid," she said. "You must teach me to whistle, it would be so useful at Covent Garden."

At the Regina it was late afternoon, the foyer softly lit, doors leading to the Grill and the Restaurant closed, the Bar doors locked, but a general activity surrounding the half dozen tea tables set in a secluded alcove. Only two were occupied and waiters hovered with laden cake trolleys.

"I should have thought all that was a waste of money," remarked Jeudwine sharply. He was walking past with Bertioni and his eyes swept over the tweed-suited woman selecting a chocolate éclair. "And very fattening," he added. "I never have understood this preoccupation for tea in this country."

Bertioni stopped, turned and walked back.

"I hope everything is to your liking, my lady," he said.

"So do I," she replied with disdain, lifting her eyes from her plate and glancing with dislike at Jeudwine's back.

Suppressing his irritation, Bertioni smiled charmingly.

"I enjoy afternoon tea, too," he said with a wistful air, "but I never seem to have the time."

He walked on, knowing the ex lady-in-waiting who had tea two or three times a week at the Regina and sometimes brought minor royalty, was looking after him with sympathy.

Bertioni was tired—not because he had spent the last two hours touring the hotel, that never tired him, but he was weary of arguing with an American who wore the jacket of his light suit too loose, and always unbuttoned, who did not know how to smoke a cigar, and who spoke too loudly. President of the Regina, maybe, Bertioni walked into the foyer with a straight back, but he has no style.

Jeudwine was ordering roses from a small counter with a token display of flowers, used by the florists as their shop window.

"Three dozen dark red and three dozen pink and send them straight away to Mrs Robin Wearne—here's the address." Jeudwine held out a card..

"We don't deliver after five." Pert, fine blonde hair falling on to her shoulders, the young assistant looked towards the clock behind the Enquiry Office desk. "And I'll have to ring the shop—I've only these few here."

"Well ring them," snapped Jeudwine, aware of Bertioni beside him. He tapped well-manicured fingers irritably on the counter.

"Your car is due in ten minutes," Bertioni was soothing, "I will just check your luggage has been collected."

He returned as the blonde, with an air of triumph, said, "Line's engaged."

Bertioni took charge. "Go on telephoning until you get through," he said sharply, "and order the roses to be ready at once. I shall send a page to collect them and deliver them to the hospital. Have you a note for Patsy?" he asked, as they walked away.

"You might have set that up," Jeudwine gave Bertioni a wry glance, then looked back over his shoulder. Bertioni had put her in her place, but he knew where he would have put her, sulky mouth, sharp little breasts thrusting through her overall.

"All the same," he said, "she is quite decorative. You might remember that when you set up your new department."

Yes, and I also remember you have a penchant for young girls behind the flowers. What was her name—Esme? Years ago, but he hasn't changed, thought Bertioni, with a grudging admiration.

"This is where we are going to have the new flower shop," he said, leading Jeudwine to the counter by the door now covered by a patchwork of airline brochures.

"Is it big enough?"

"Oh, yes, we can build out if need be, but there is this space at the back." Bertioni opened a small half door, "which will give us plenty of room."

"And stop your staff using it to dump their bags," Jeudwine pointed to the airline bag pushed under the back of the counter. Well, he'd won a point at last, a small one, but he knew by the stiffening of Bertioni's shoulders that it was one that mattered.

For the second time within the last half hour Bertioni felt fatigued and irritated. Jeudwine, however, was jaunty, at least he'd found one thing, though small, that was not quite perfect in this so perfect old-fashioned hotel.

"Goodbye, Carlo," he said, smiling widely, "I shall send Jan Vitold over after he's finished with the accountants in Paris. He'll get you off the hook with your florist's tenancy and you'll get me off the hook with Jan. Right?"

Andrew, who had been hovering for some time, watched them leave the warm foyer for the November dark outside. He turned his attention to the ticker tape for the few more minutes of waiting and saw the typed words run ahead ... "IRA say they plan a new offensive in London ..."

God, I hate them. Andrew turned and saw Bertioni stride through the doors looking as furious as he felt himself.

What's upset the old man, he wondered, walking towards him.

"Mr Bertioni," he said, "I'm afraid I've been chasing you all day—I really do need your advice."

Bertioni gave a little shrug of his shoulders as if to throw away tension and his hard face softened. Smiling, he said, "Yes, I know, I'm sorry, I've been rather tied up with our revered President. I'll join you in five minutes." He looked up at the clock, nearly six, and in a few minutes new staff would take over; dinner jackets for the receptionists, the bar would open and the Regina would begin its evening life.

"A whisky and soda wouldn't come amiss," he said, and Andrew nodded, turning back to his office and wondering why Bertioni was delving behind the desk that held the travel pamphlets. He would soon hear, and yes, a Scotch was a good idea, it had been a long day.

The bag could not contain food, there was a staff canteen, or tights or whatever the girls wore, for they had their own changing rooms. It could only mean, Bertioni thought, bending down, suspicious, something stolen so that it could be hurried out through the front door instead of the security of the staff entrance. With this in mind, he picked it up, surprised by its weight, saw the wires protruding from the half zipped up opening, and heard for a brief second the ticking of a clock, before it was submerged by the laughter and raised voices behind him, party sounds, guests arriving for an evening of pleasure, jostling through the swing doors.

Bertioni stood up, holding the bag stiffly in front of him. There was a small side door which porters used beside the Front entrance and he hurried through. Outside two taxis were drawn up and there was bustle, porters carrying luggage, and he slipped unseen into the shadowy road and across to the gardens. The gates would be locked, but if there was time, and his heart was loud in his ears, he could throw it over the railings.

Bertioni was tired, but he lifted the bag and threw it with all the force he could muster in to the gardens, away from his hotel and all who were in it. It hit the first tree, there was a blinding flash, a great roar of explosion and force that carried Bertioni backwards to fling him against the wall of the Regina. As his limp body fell to the pavement, there was a tinkle of glass, falling like rain.

ELEVEN

Vitold was waiting, as Louise knew he would be, under the harsh yellow overhead lights, hatless, in a short dark overcoat. His smile was at once warm and relieved, then he took control.

Luggage, passport, taxi, suddenly she was being driven at great speed towards Paris, everything taken care of, solicitous care, but no kiss of greeting.

"You are so discreet, Vitold," teased Louise.

The speed as they rounded a corner threw her suddenly against him. "Oh," she laughed, "I'd forgotten how frantic driving in Paris can be."

"*Moja kochana*," holding her closely, Vitold kissed her cheek and Louise put her head on his shoulder.

After a while she sat up, leaning forward on the edge of the leather seat, passing lights catching her fair hair, the eager lift of her chin. She was in Paris with Vitold, dear, serious, handsome Vitold. The taxi sped down the Champs Elysees, passing lights flicked like small fireworks, horns shrilled, brakes squealed, there was an air of great expectancy.

"Oh, my dear Polish friend," Louise turned to kiss him, a caress of scented hair, the scent evocative, uncatchable, transient—like Louise, thought Vitold, who had been watching her.

Never the time and the place and the loved one altogether, Browning's lines. Perhaps it was better that way, then one could always dream and think of what might have been. When it happened, when the time and the place and the loved one were now, how easy to fail the moment.

Vitold looked out of the window.

"We are nearly there," he said, "but we are not stopping. I shall leave your suitcase, which I have arranged to be unpacked, then we shall go to the Ritz to drink champagne."

Louise looked at him, surprised.

"The reason being that once we step inside the Hotel Josephine there will be a reception committee for you, champagne with the Manager, followed by a lengthy banquet, where I shall be seated at the bottom of the table. Afterwards there will be a tour of the hotel and I shall not have been alone with you for the whole evening."

Laughing, Louise saw in the light from the portico as they drew up that Vitold was smiling at her rather shyly.

"So you cancelled it all?"

Vitold nodded.

"Then can we go to the George V instead?"

"Happy memories?" asked Vitold later, as they sat on gilt chairs in a secluded corner of the bar.

He spoke lightly but Louise recognised the question in the deep set eyes, dark eyes that could change so quickly. How difficult love is, one expects it to be at the peak of happiness all the time and yet there is always a little whisper of doubt to be heard faintly if you are listening for it. And Vitold is listening, wondering who I came with and who gave me the silver chain.

Louise lifted her glass of champagne.

"Nasdrovia," she said, she was smiling at him.

"With father, of course. I told you how we came to Paris together ..."

"Yes, and talked French all the time."

"Well, not all the time, especially when he gave me this silver chain with the little mother of pearl crucifix. I couldn't keep on saying 'Milles mercies' for ever, and I didn't know what it was in French."

"Chain is the same, crucifix is the same, argent for silver, nacre is mother of pearl—now put it all together." Vitold's eyes were now light with amusement.

"No prep tonight," Louise laughed at him. "And, please,

another favour, dear Polish friend. Can we have dinner at one of those bistros with a menu outside in faded violet ink?"

Vitold, who had booked a table at Maxim's, looked at her quizzically.

"When did you ever go to a bistro?" he asked.

"Never. That's the whole point. When I've been in Paris with Adrian and Tom, Adrian wants to go to the Ritz, Tom likes the Scribe and we stay at the Lancaster—so we spend all our time rushing round the streets looking for each other. That's when I used to look at the little places and I would think of you and your flat above the breakfast café. I've always wanted to go to a bistro, but only with you. And it must have red and white checked tablecloths," she said, shrugging her shoulders, her head tilted towards him, wide mouth smiling. "Please."

Vitold, having telephoned Maxims to cancel the table, the order for caviare in pastry boats, the little baskets of wild strawberries, found Louise waiting for him in the wide empty foyer, wearing her white trenchcoat with the natural arrogance he knew and loved.

Outside a faint rain was falling and Vitold signalled for a taxi, but Louise shook her head and, taking his hand, began to walk. A slippery sticky rain with the smoky smell of petrol fumes caught in the dampness of wet paving stones.

"Oh, it's lovely, the smell of Paris—even the rain has a scent all its own." Louise stopped beneath a street light, pulled a scarf from her pocket and tied it peasant fashion round her hair.

"Now I am a Polish peasant and you are my Polish lover. You are a labourer who works in the fields all day and makes love to me all night."

When Vitold laughed, suddenly, spontaneously, it was a very boyish laugh.

"Then I know one Polish labourer who will not do a very good day's work tomorrow!"

They came to the Seine, damp leaves, pale and trodden into a matted surface, silenced their footsteps.

"We are walking along the banks of the Vistula. Does it run through the centre of Warsaw like the Seine runs through Paris?"

"The Vistula runs between Warsaw and Praga," Vitold was happy to answer her question and waved his hand in the direction of the shadowy water.

"We are two lovers walking along the Warsaw bank. Across the river is Praga—and your labouring friend is very hungry."

"You once said I ate like a peasant . . . years ago, the first meal we ever had together . . ."

"At Claridge's in the Causerie, and you kept going round and round the centre table piling your plate with hors d'oeuvres . . ."

"And I found Polish sausage," Louise interrupted in her light happy voice. "Do you remember?"

"Do I remember, *moja kochana*? I remember everything we have ever said together or ever shared together."

"I think I am a very young Polish peasant." Louise stopped in a pool of lamplight. "I keep wanting to kiss you in that uncomplicated way that teenagers do."

The rain had stopped and she pulled off her scarf, the hand she held to him, gloveless and chilled. Vitold held it against his cheek, staring into the water beyond.

"The ink is not violet, nor faded, but it is quite shabby. Will it do?"

Standing together, they peered at the brightly lit menu in its plastic case, above them a faded striped awning.

"Lovely smells and they've got *rognons*, my favourite. I shall have salad Niçoise first. Please, Vitold," said Louise, "let's go in here."

"You should, as a Polish peasant girl, be eating beetroot and dumplings," Vitold replied severely, but with the indulgent smile she knew so well.

Inside it was warm and noisy, snatches of song, an accordian played by a bearded youth in a dark beret, orders shouted through a distant hatchway with a theatrical fervour. Everything was done at great speed. A bottle of white wine and two glasses placed on the table, bowls of salad, rolls, butter before the aproned waiter would discuss their main dish.

"It's all faster than the speed of sound," said Louise happily. "I do think we ought to bring Mr Raymond here—one waits for ever in the Grill sometimes."

"The whole idea," said Vitold, filling her glass, "is to put food on the table immediately because the more you eat the more you drink. It is as simple as that." He watched Louise's bright, lively gaze as she looked round the room.

"I am sorry there are no red and white tablecloths, but white ones are more Polish. On Christmas Eve we always have a party, it is a special day for us, and we have a big table with a white cloth and underneath the table we place a bale of hay."

His smile was depletory, as if inviting her to smile at such foolishness, but Louise knew the yearning in those dark eyes and touched his hand.

"Tell me about Christmas in Poland," she said, as if she was asking for a bedtime story.

"The hay is in memory of the Manger," said Vitold quietly, and there was a faraway look in his deep eyes. "Sometimes in the country they put a sheaf of wheat so that there will be good harvests in the coming year. And when the first star shows in the sky, to remind us of the Star of Bethlehem, we all sit down to supper, the master with his servants and the officers with their men. For this is the Polish tradition, and this is the most enjoyed meal of the year, and always there is one empty place left so that if a traveller should arrive on our Holy night he will be welcomed."

> *Is there anybody there? said the traveller,*
> *Knocking on the moonlit door . . .*

"I've always loved that poem," Louise quoted, "and now I know why. Go on, Vitold."

"There is a big Christmas tree by the table, decorated with lights, and under it are all the presents. But first we have supper made from twelve meatless dishes, it is very traditional.

136

After that we open our presents and sing Polish songs and then, in this happy loving mood, we go outside and make our way to the Midnight Mass. It is our best day in the whole year."

Vitold turned to Louise who was looking at him quietly, her chin resting on her hand, and he saw she loved him.

It is all in the present, she thought, as if Christmas happens in Poland every year for him.

"I remember it all from *Soldier Bear*," she said, "your Polish Christmas and how you created it in the desert and how Voytek got away and ate all the fruit. Dear Voytek, I would have loved him even though he was six foot tall!"

"I cherish that book so much," Vitold spoke quietly. "I take it with me everywhere. It is upstairs now in my room at the hotel. It is for so many reasons that I cherish it—for General Anders and the 2nd Polish Corps, because you gave it to me, and for the inscription ..."

"I wanted to write so much more," interrupted Louise, "something very loving."

"You did write something very loving—'To V from MK' What could be more loving than *moja kochana*? And for so many other reasons it is most dear to me. There is an introduction to *Soldier Bear* which I know by heart. Can I say it to you?"

"Please, Vitold."

"The knife edge between victory and defeat, both in war and peace, usually depends upon how people use their emotions. Computers cannot control these emotions. However well equipped we may be, it is left to each one of us to find that extra something which makes the difference between losing and winning. Voytek in his strange way harnessed the emotions of the soldiers around him so that he became a symbol of the love for their families and faraway homeland."

Vitold hesitated, his eyes very bright.

"That is why the authorities allowed him to stay. That is why the men of General Anders' army cared for, laughed at, fought with, took courage from ... Voytek, Soldier Bear."

137

Louise lifted her glass.

"To Voytek," she said gently, "and to your Poland."

They were silent for a while, a shared companionable silence, and then Louise said wistfully:

"I wish we were going back to your little flat. How I missed it after you had gone. I used to go there and stand looking up at the wooden steps until one day a West Indian woman opened the door and shouted at me. I went once again after that, one damp wet afternoon on my way back to our new house in Hertfordshire and a vandal had uprooted the bay tree and thrown it in a corner by the dustbins from the café. It was very tired, the leaves all curled and dry, but I picked it up and took it back to where I was parked and put it in the boot of my car, and when I got home I took a torch and went and planted it down by the stream. Of course it didn't live, it was like one of those Christmas trees that they have cut the roots off, and you plant it hopefully because you want it to go on, but the needles turn brown and fall. That is what happened to our little bay tree, it turned brown and died. There is still a little wooden stick there—I go often to look at it."

"You loved the anonymity of that flat, didn't you? I loved it too, it was the only home of my own I have ever had. In America I have an executive suite in all the Lincoln Hotels as I rush from one to the other, but no place of my own. I have a record player in my New York suite and sometimes I play Dvorak's *New World Symphony* and wonder why he embraced the new world so much. I do not embrace it at all."

"Could you come back to England—to us?" began Louise, only to be halted by the flourish of aromatic plates, more wine, a voluble exchange by the waiter with Vitold, who sipped the red wine, and nodded acceptance.

"Oh, you've got *pommes frites* with your steak." Louise eyed Vitold's plate, and he smiled and held one to her mouth.

"Why is it they taste so good in France?" Louise rubbed her lips. "And now I want your watercress," she laughed at him.

"Impossible."

"You can have some of my rognons . . . "

"*C'est bon.*"

It was a statement of fact from the aproned waiter as he filled their glasses.

Vitold tasted a piece of kidney from Louise's plate.

"*Oui,*" he looked up, "*il est excellent.*"

"Now my watercress!" Louise demanded, happy, secure, uncomplicated. She has a pretty smile noted the waiter.

"*Voulez-vous des petit pois ou du chou-fleur?*" he asked Vitold, who had carefully chosen a sprig of watercress from his steak and held it out to Louise.

"*Donnez-m'en tres peu,*" he replied without looking up.

"*Qui?*" Then getting no answer, the waiter shrugged his shoulders and spooned both peas and cauliflower on to Vitold's plate.

Foreigners were mad, and when they were in love they were very mad, but Madame was enchanting and Monsieur's French was good and he had great style.

Louise tested the creamy dish before her.

"*Je les aime beaucoup,*" she said, smiling at him.

"There goes one happy waiter," said Vitold, "I believe he would rather have your approval than a good tip."

"Enough French for one evening." Louise sipped her wine. "What were we talking about before all this delicious food and drink arrived?"

"My coming back to London."

"Oh, could you?" Louise put down her fork and looked up, eyes wide with appeal in an earnest face. "You could find another flat and life would begin all over again."

"Only if I'm fired, I suppose." Vitold shrugged his shoulders. "I rather think the President is getting a little tired of what he calls my 'cloistered' mind. It is good that I can do the sums so well when he is buying and selling, but he is so anxious to prove that he is still virile, that only youth pleases him now and he has a young nephew, very clean-cut Yale young man, who says and does all the right things." His eyes crinkled with amusement. "Do you still *aime beaucoup* your kidneys in cream sauce?" he teased.

"Don't change the subject, *moja kochana*, I do want you to come back so much."

"No, no, little peasant girl—your pronunciation is nearly as bad as your French. Try again—moiya cohahna ..." Louise repeated it after him, slowly.

"Polish is such a difficult language," she sighed.

The waiter, passing, hearing her sigh and watching as she touched the man's cheek, stopped and refilled both their glasses. They did not notice and he went on his way. Elegant people. There would be a good tip. He kept an eye on them. No coffee, no brandy. When they'd finished their meal and were leaving, he saw them to the door.

"*Revenez bientot*," he called, folding the notes into his pocket.

"Are we a long way from the Champs Elysees?"

"No, very near."

"Can we walk there and see all the lights?"

"We shall do that and have some brandy."

"But outside, Vitold, on the pavement."

"You will feel cold and the chairs will be damp, but you are so warm with love you do not mind, is that what you are saying?" He was teasing her again.

"Yes, that is what I am saying." Louise tucked her arm through his, "also I don't like brandy."

"I remember, but you shall have something very special as befits a Princess—it is called Mirabelle brandy—made from little yellow plums."

The Hotel Josephine was subdued when they returned. Lights were dimmed and one elderly concierge stood behind the desk as Vitold collected the keys.

"There is a message upstairs for you," he said.

Vitold had been awake for a long time. He lay on his side, released and content, his arm around Louise, curled like a small animal with her back to him. In all the years they had never spent a whole night together. He had not known that she liked only one pillow—the other tossed unceremoniously on to the floor. That she was afraid of the dark and the heavy satin curtains had to be drawn back to show a pale square of light. He had not known that after the first love-making, she could laugh and chatter like a child, and then, suddenly silent, would caress him expertly for further love making, and after a sigh of pleasure, fall quickly, deeply asleep. What he had known, in all the years, was that to be with Louise made him come alive again. She made the present more important than the past. The past he was still trying to forget, the future he did not wish to probe into too deeply. Now was the only important time, if you did not get it right it haunted you, and if you wasted it looking ahead to something that could never happen, then you wasted it too.

Vitold opened his eyes and saw the grey square of window had become a little lighter. Tomorrow, he thought sleepily, no, today, it was after dawn, he had to meet the accountants and take over the hotel. His conscience prodded him that he had forgotten something, but he felt quite lighthearted about it. Nothing mattered except the scent of the hair on the pillow beside him.

TWELVE

Street sounds awoke Vitold car horns, the acceleration of engines, sudden shrill calls and an odd monotonous knocking as if building was in progress. For a moment in the grey light he wondered, then his hand felt the soft skin beside him and, with the touch, the awareness that all the romantic dreamings over the years, were true, were now. He longed to waken her and tell her, but as he lay there hesitating he knew that something was troubling him, that same niggle of conscience. Then he remembered. Last night he had not gone back to his room to read the message left for him.

"Don't go—I can't spare you for a second." Louise had nuzzled her face against his. "Please, darling, it can only be from old Jeudwine who is halfway across the Atlantic ..."

"A little further, I think."

"Well, wherever he is, he wouldn't expect you to answer at this hour and it's so lovely. This dear doll-like little sitting room with the gilt and satin sofa, so spindly and unsafe to sit on." She had bounced on it, laughing. "Do you think it would hold Mr Jeudwine?" Voice light with pleasure, running through to the bedroom to come back dancing:

"Dear one, you'll never guess—it's a real old-fashioned double bed with carved ends and they've turned the sheets down on both sides!"

"Of course, we are in Paris."

"Oh, why do the French think they invented love?" Louise had said impatiently. "Here are red roses, my own special scent and a Hermes scarf in a pretty box tied with brown satin ribbon, all given me by my lover, who is very Polish."

142

She had put her arms round his neck.

"I do love you, you know."

Now, in the misty greyness of early morning, Vitold dressed in the small sitting room. He had drawn the heavy satin curtains, but had not put on the light. On the small table against the wall with its marble top and gilded cupboard beneath, the bottle of champagne he had ordered listed sideways in the tepid water that had once been ice. Vitold picked an apple from the basket of fruit beside it, smiling. They had not needed champagne. He bit into the apple, found it soft and flaccid, and left it on the plate, dipped his hands in the finger bowl and dried them on the neatly folded napkin. Now he picked up the two sets of keys and walked to the door. He would come back again and they could have breakfast together. The warm sweet scent of flowers had brushed him as he passed, and now he stopped, walked back and picked one rose from the bowl, wiped the stem and walked softly back into the bedroom. Louise lay on her back, sleeping, one hand resting on the pillow, palm uppermost. Vitold stood quietly then placed the rose against her hand. Louise did not move.

Vitold walked up the stairs to his room and, as he opened the door he saw the small envelope on the mat. It was marked URGENT.

'Please telephone immediately. Very urgent. Andrew Merrin.'

Vitold looked for the time. '6.45 pm last night'. They had been at the George V—something had happened to Jeudwine. A plane crash? They had heard no news, engulfed in their own happy world. He put through the call, asked the exchange to ring back and walked nervously up and down the room. Then he went into the bedroom, searching in his suitcase for the cigarettes Louise was chiding him to give up. The neat unslept-in bed had a cold virginal look and he thumped the pillow impatiently, ruffling the sheets as if by his guilt he could make them appear used. The insistent peal of the telephone bell caused him to drop his cigarette in the ashtray on the bedside table and run back to the sitting room.

"Vitold?" Andrew's voice. "I have been trying to get you since last night. Where have you been?"

"I only just this minute got your message," began Vitold . . .

"Never mind about that, I have very bad news." The voice was drained, tired. "Yesterday we had an IRA bomb planted in the foyer and Mr Bertioni found it and ran outside with it to throw it away and save the hotel. If he had waited and we had called the police he might have been saved, who knows, but his instinct was to save his hotel. It hit a tree in the gardens and went off. He was blown backwards with force against the wall of the Regina. He died immediately."

Vitold did not speak. "Oh, Louise, Louise, my darling."

"Vitold are you there?" The line crackled, the voice irritated with strain.

"Yes, I am sorry. I am so shocked that I find it very difficult —I am so shocked . . ."

"We all are, in fact we are distraught." The tired voice hesitated with emotion. "But the worst thing is to tell Louise— Lady Wearne. You will have to do it, Vitold. The Chairman decided we couldn't do it by telephone—it was such a special relationship . . ."

"I know . . ." Vitold's voice was almost inaudible.

"Are you there? This is an awfully bad line. Look, Vitold, will you tell her—God, I don't envy you," here the voice sighed, "but she must come back straight away. Will you organise it and let me know the time. I know you can't leave with your schedule, but I'll get my wife to meet her."

Vitold put down the receiver and went back to the bedroom to find his cigarette. It had fallen from the ashtray on to the pale carpet and there was the acrid smell of scorched wool. Bertioni would never have been so careless. Bertioni . . . Vitold closed his eyes and gave a deep shuddering sigh, then he forced himself to take command. He telephoned the airport, ordered coffee, ran a bath and dressed in a plain suit with a dark tie, left a message with the hotel Manager that he would be detained for a while . . . all of this he did without feeling, his mind numb. At last he knew he could put the moment off

144

no longer. It was after nine o'clock. Vitold stood up, squared his shoulders, picked up the keys and went out into the passage.

Vitold opened the sitting-room door and saw the remains of breakfast on the white-clothed table, an empty cup of coffee, a half finished brioche and was suddenly afraid. The complimentary morning newspaper, supposing she had read it and had found out on her own. The bedroom door was ajar and he knocked gently. Louise was standing by the bed in a white satin slip edged with lace, fastening a suspender, pale wing of hair falling against her bare shoulder.

"Oh, hulloa, darling. I'm so glad you're back. I missed you so much when I woke up that I had to get up straight away. It's a lovely day, lots of blue sky and I'm going out to buy you a present before I do my tour of the hotel."

She came towards him, slipping her arms round his neck.

"Have I had a kiss this morning? The rose was a kiss, of course, how dear of you. I am going to press it and keep it for ever and ever until I am a very old lady."

Only then, as she brushed her cheek against his, was Louise aware of Vitold's quietness. He had not spoken since he returned and he stood with a martial stiffness that alarmed her.

"Something is wrong," she said, in a small frightened voice, standing back and looking up into Vitold's face. He seemed to be struggling for control, eyes squeezed shut.

"Yes, something is very wrong, my darling," he said gently, leading her to the bed, sitting down beside her and cradling her with his arm.

He picked up her hand.

"Yesterday evening a bomb was left at the Regina and your father found it and took it outside and threw it in the gardens, but ..." Vitold hesitated, then hurried on, "it exploded and ..." his arm tightened round her ... "and your father was killed ..."

"Oh, no, ... oh, no, that couldn't happen—it couldn't, it couldn't, it couldn't ..."

It seemed to Vitold, holding Louise, that life had suddenly

145

ebbed from her, leaving a still cold statue. He took off his jacket and wrapped it round her and still she sat looking down at her clasped hands, not moving, until she was overcome by shivering so violent that Vitold, alarmed, hurried next door and came back with a glass of brandy. He held it to her lips and Louise sipped mechanically, like a small child ordered to take medicine. After a while the shivering subsided and Louise lay back on the pillows, her eyes closed.

Looking down at the still face resting against his jacket, all the loving and giving and infectious joy of life wiped away, Vitold was overwhelmed by the depth of his love. Coloured slides across his memory, hovered for a second, then flicked away.

Louise in the bomb-damaged pub on the river, smiling at him for the first time.

Louise running laughing up the wooden steps to his flat and emerging fluffy haired from his steamy bathroom.

Dancing in a mackintosh and head scarf in the rain under the floodlights at the Festival of Britain and insisting the Skylon was an exclamation mark, written on the night sky by a surprised God.

Wandering hand in hand along the river bank to Kew on his day off and sitting on a seat in the warm spring sunshine beneath a cascade of pink blossom, listening to a nearby grass cutter and smelling the fresh green scent.

"They have made the Skylon into ashtrays—I shall buy one for you," head on one side, eyes crinkled in merriment, "they're probably repellant ..."

Laughter was always lurking round the wide generous mouth, in her large brown eyes.

"You're such a serious old bear, a honey coloured Syrian bear who wants lots of love."

"Yes, please." He had stroked her hair gently and she had turned and smiled, then concentrated solemnly on her driving. One of his visits from America and she had met him at a drab country station in a station wagon with a golden retriever, lolling tongue, ingratiating, on the back seat.

146

"We're going to Whipsnade," she'd said in her light musical voice, "to find Voytek. But first I must give mine lots of love."

She had stopped then, in a shaded lane, June trees dappled the grass, the dog, released, ran barking into the unknown and Louise, Louise was wearing something very soft and easy to move.

Once, knowing he was coming to the Regina, she had met him at Heathrow, wearing a strawberry-coloured fitted coat, six inches above her knees, long slim legs, expensive black shoes, flat with little bows on the front.

"I'm anonymous," she had laughed, greeting him, unaware of the effect of a happy person, bright as an exotic bird, among the drab duffle coats, the jeans and large striped running shoes.

Now Vitold packed neatly and quickly with the expertise of one who has done it many times, wrapping shoes in tissue paper then walking to the bathroom to collect her tooth brush and the little sponge she always used. When he returned he saw the bed was empty and Louise was dressed, wearing a grey suit with a white fur collar that accentuated her pallor. She was collecting her jewellery from the dressing table and putting it into a velvet case, the last to be put away was the silver chain with its little pearl crucifix.

The telephone rang to say the car was waiting and Vitold closed the suitcase, then opened the door and found the porter waiting. When he turned for Louise he found she had gone back to the dressing table to collect the red rose which she had placed in her tooth glass, and she looked at him, her lips trembling in a sad attempt to smile. Vitold took her arm and turned away his head, for more than anything else the valiant little effort twisted his heart and he found his eyes bright with tears.

Downstairs, the Manager hovered discreetly by the door, but Vitold gave an almost imperceptible shake of his head and he did not come forward. In the car Louise sat on the edge of the seat with a straight back, looking down. She had

147

not spoken since that first frantic cry and Vitold was afraid. I have not told her very well. Now he leaned forward and, putting his hand under her chin, turned her face gently.

"You are my one and only love," he said, and felt the warm tears on his hand.

"Oh, Vitold, how am I going to . . ." she did not finish the sentence but buried her head in his shoulder. Holding her tightly, Vitold felt with his free hand for his handkerchief and gave it to her, all the time murmuring endearments, grateful for the normality of tears. After a while her sobbing ceased and she lay quite still as if asleep.

Vitold looked at his watch.

"We are nearly there, *moja kochana*," he whispered.

Louise gave a faint sigh and sat up, feeling for her handbag. Vitold, looking out of the window, saw they were approaching the airport.

"Give me your passport," he said, "and I will take care of everything." He saw she had powdered her face and was wearing a pair of dark glasses.

It was a very still morning. Even the sounds and bustle of traffic and people seemed curiously remote, the brash noise of a record that could be turned off at will. A pale sunlight washed across the sky, a sky so pale a blue that it was lost in the distance.

Louise was the last to board the plane. The dark glasses made her small heart-shaped face seem smaller, and Vitold, bending to kiss her cheek, whispered:

"Be brave, *moja kochana*."

At the bottom of the steps he saw her pause, straighten her shoulders and tilt her proud head. Bertioni's daughter, still clutching his crumpled handkerchief, was going home.

Vitold turned and walked away, back to the waiting car.

"The Hotel Josephine," he said, opening the door, "as quick as you can."

As he sat down, he saw across the leather seat a scattering of rose petals.